Charley Feather

Also by Kate Pennington

Tread Softly
Brief Candle

Charley Feather

Kate Pennington

Hodder
Children's
Books

a division of Hodder Headline Limited

A Catalogue record for this book is available from the British Library

ISBN 0 340 87873 8

Typeset in Garamond by Avon DataSet Ltd,
Bidford-on-Avon, Warwickshire

Printed and bound in Great Britain by
Bookmarque Ltd, Croydon, Surrey

The paper and board used in this paperback by Hodder Children's Books
are natural recyclable products made from wood grown in sustainable forests.
The manufacturing processes conform to the environmental
regulations of the country of origin.

Hodder Children's Books
a division of Hodder Headline Limited
338 Euston Road
London NW1 3BH

The Highwayman

He'd a French cocked hat on his forehead, a bunch of lace
  at his chin,
A coat of claret velvet, and breeches of brown doe-skin.
They fitted with never a wrinkle. His boots were up to the
  thigh.
And he rode with a jewelled twinkle,
His pistol butts a-twinkle
His rapier hilt a-twinkled, under the jewelled sky.

Alfred Noyes

Saturday 7 April, 1739

I've seen eight men hanged. Today will be my ninth.

They usually die game, confessing their sins before they're turned off the ladder. Then they kick and struggle, they may foam at the mouth for a full half hour before they die.

And yet sometimes they cut the man down and find he has life in him yet; my friend, O'Neill, sprang up as they were nailing down his coffin and lives to this day. He's one of the half-hanged – some would say the luckiest man alive.

No, don't turn away. Life for we thieves (for that is what I am) is often brutal and short; our last gasp dangling on the end of a rope is done to please the crowd.

As I say before, I've seen eight men hanged, but none approach it like the great Dick Turpin. They call him the most famous highwayman in all England. And yet what was he, when all is said and done? A mere butcher by trade, and no gentleman stealing from the rich to give to the poor.

I'm standing in the cold rain on the edge of the Knavesmire, a mile outside the city of York, watching as Turpin is carried in a cart from the county gaol, up Micklegate, through Micklegate Bar.

'Turpin is game!' the crowd around me cry. He bows and waves as he passes. He wears a new green coat and pumps and has shared amongst his mourners three pounds and ten shillings.

It's no less than you would expect.

Now the cart trundles into sight. There's a great yell and much pushing, and, as I've not yet reached my full height, I'm shoved backwards, almost losing my hat. I jam it back on my head and find myself crushed against one of the legs of the gallows, squinting up at the noose.

It's a prime spot, as it happens.

I see Turpin swagger down from the cart and control a trembling of his left leg by stamping his foot before he mounts the ladder. The hangman places the noose around his neck. Then Turpin gazes about him, head up, shoulders squared to face what he must. He speaks boldly with the executioner.

'I leave a gold ring and two pairs of shoes to Mrs Ginny Jonson in the town of Brough,' he declares. 'And my hatbands and gloves to Charles Carr of York.'

This is good stuff. The crowd loves it.

I stand under the gallows in my boy's breeches and waistcoat and my three-cornered hat. I feel the wind cut through me.

Turpin looks down and I fancy he catches my eye. My face may be the last thing on this cold earth that he sees as, suddenly and as though merely straddling a horse to go on a journey, he throws himself from the ladder.

One

*In which Turpin's body is conveyed to the tavern
and I reflect upon man's mortality. I beat a cold retreat
to the Blue Boar and here you meet my confederates.
But then more pressing matters intervene.*

'How was the hanging, Charley?' Mary Brazier pounced on me the minute I entered the Blue Boar. She doesn't attend these occasions herself, being superstitious.

I escaped her embrace and sat down all of a cold tremble by the fire. 'The crowd hung on his legs to speed the matter. He croaked after five minutes,' I said.

'Blessed release,' Mary muttered, crossing herself. 'I wager he went with a swagger, though?'

I recalled those cold, dark eyes piercing me with his last gaze. Master Butcher. Lord of the Highways. 'He put on a good show,' I agreed, teeth chattering.

Mary stroked her plump, pink neck then shuddered. She stared hard at me in the light of the flickering flames. 'You're a cold fish, you are, Charley Feather.'

I shrugged. 'The mare he stole was worth three

pounds, and the foal twenty shillings. I wouldn't risk my neck for less than twenty guineas.'

'Heartless, considering your tender age.' Mary sniffed, turning to O'Neill, my half-hanged friend. 'Ain't he, Patrick? I'm saying, ain't young Charley an unfeeling swine, going up the Knavesmire to enjoy the spectacle of poor Dick Turpin dancing his final jig from the Three-legged Mare?'

Truth is, I'm not the cold fish that Mary makes me out to be. But I reckon that seeing a man hang sharpens my wits. I'll think harder and run quicker in future, and make sure to avoid the drop.

Patrick O'Neill grunted into his pewter pot. His voice never recovered from his brush with the hangman's noose. When he speaks, the words issue from his throat in a strangulated whisper.

It was Mary Brazier who paid the men to cut O'Neill down from the gallows before he had quite croaked. She'd met him first in Newgate Gaol and taken a shine to him, though God knows why. The man's ugly, broad face is livid and scarred with the smallpox. He was once a farrier in Tadcaster, but turned to stealing horses, and from there went wholly to the bad. I know never to get on the wrong side of O'Neill, believe me.

'Oh, Charley.' Mary sighed, stroking my smooth cheek with the back of her hand. 'And did you bring me back anything pleasant from your morning jaunt?'

I sighed back at her, rolling my eyes and looking to the heavens. 'It was too cold and wet to work,' I teased, then pulled out of my waistcoat pocket a fob watch on a heavy gold chain. I put it down on the oak board for Mary to examine.

A smile creased her face. 'There was gentry at the Knavesmire, then?'

'A knight, two baronets and a justice of the peace,' I reported faithfully.

'Why only the one watch, then?' O'Neill hissed, glowering at me with his nasty, rheumy eyes.

I scowled and pulled out a silver pill-box and a couple of silk handkerchiefs.

'That's the lot!' I vowed, keeping to myself the small gold locket I had slipped from around the pretty neck of a girl my own age.

I see you despise me, and in your shoes, who can blame you? But I was born to this, and know nothing else.

'Charley, Charley . . .' Mary sighed again.

Somebody called for more drink and Mary whipped up the watch, the pill-box and handkerchiefs, stuffed them down the bodice of her red dress and ran for ale.

It is Wild, the leader of more than one hundred gangs, who has called for drink.

I mean Thomas Wild, only son of Jonathan Wild –

the great pickpocket, cutpurse, housebreaker, shoplifter, fraudster and general man of violence. There was no dark business that Wild Senior did not attempt and, as everyone knows, for two decades he escaped each time with a clean pair of heels.

Young Thomas spent his boyhood watching his father's crooked empire grow. At the last, Jonathan was employing great gangs who lifted silver plates from churches, jewels from around the necks of court ladies, papers from bankers worth thousands of guineas.

Thomas's job, when he grew to be a man, was to hide Jonathan's ill-gotten gains in a great warehouse by the river, then ship it out to Holland where it was sold. Truly, Thomas had learned his craft from a master.

The old man's luck finally ran out, though, and they hanged him at Tyburn. (I missed this particular hanging, for it was 1725 and I am, so far as I can tell, coming up fourteen years of age, though you would take me for less by my size and stature.)

Then Thomas came into his own.

The London gangs carried on bringing booty to the heir apparent from Charing Cross and St Pancras, Southwark and Holborn; watches, seals, snuff-boxes, rings. If men crossed Thomas Wild, he betrayed them to the justices, just like his father before him. For Thomas is a chip off the old block – an agent, a forger, a fence.

And what have I to do with Thomas Wild?

Well, it is through Mary Brazier and O'Neill that I come under Wild's shadow. O'Neill is his long-time confederate, and I was taken up by Mary some three winters past, when she found me starving by the river and thought she might put me to some use by and by.

O'Neill and Mary have been married a year last January, she having carelessly lost two husbands before – one by hanging, one shot dead by a rival.

So chance, and starvation, put me in the way of my present trade, which is the same as the late, lamented Turpin. That is, I am a highwayman on the roads between York and London, a member of one of Wild's gangs, and they named me Charley Feather for the great, curved plume of feathers I wear in my hat, and for the lightness of my touch.

I am nigh on fourteen years of age, as I said before, and carry with me a great secret, which I will share with no man.

But how came I to be starving on the bank of the great River Thames in the shadow of Westminster? Well, more of that after I tell you what took place when Wild called for ale at the Blue Boar Inn on Castlegate.

Wild doesn't travel with us unless he has business in York. This is as well; his presence makes us edgy, and our gang leader, Claude Delamere – known as Frenchy

– must sit in Wild's shadow, lest the great man judge him too big for his supple boots.

'Drink up, Delamere!' Wild ordered while Mary hurried to top up supplies.

O'Neill kept his head down, intent on the playing cards he was dealing with his thick fingers. Frenchy drained his pot. He took his hand of cards from O'Neill with a quiet smile. Wild surveyed our fellow drinkers through a fug of smoke and steam. 'Where's that damned Hind?' he cried out. 'Why is he not here as arranged?'

'Patience,' Mary advised, putting fresh ale down in front of him.

But patience is not a virtue of Thomas Wild's, as well we knew. I sat hugging the fire, keeping out of it.

'Is it Jasper Hind you mean?' a man by the door inquired. 'I saw him at the Knavesmire, showing a keen interest in Turpin's leavetaking.'

'Aye, Jasper Hind,' Wild snarled, snatching up his own hand of cards from the board. 'I have business with him.'

The game continued, with Frenchy throwing down the queen of hearts and telling Mary with a grin that he had no need of that card, since she was already his very own queen of hearts, which naturally provoked O'Neill into a hissing growl. It's Frenchy's way with the women to be charming and shallow, and mean nothing. But

Mary laughed and pulled her red bodice straight and twisted a lock of hair around her finger.

Then Hind arrived at last – a small man with stooping shoulders and hands too big for his twisted body.

'Jasper, you've kept Mister Wild waiting!' the man at the door hailed him. 'He's out of temper, you mark my words.'

And Wild's face did indeed look dark, as if brooding over some serious wrong.

Some of the men in the room fell quiet as Hind took off his hat and advanced, saddlebag slung across his shoulder. But for some minutes Wild went on playing his game of cards, and Hind's coat, wet from the rain storm which battered at the window of the Blue Boar, began to steam. His white scalp gleamed through the damp strands of dark hair.

'You come straight from the Knavesmire?' Frenchy asked him eventually, to break the mood.

'Aye. The crowd was very great,' Hind replied uneasily. 'The corpse follows fast upon my heels.'

'Does it indeed?' Frenchy cried, looking up from the game. 'They bring Turpin here, to the Blue Boar?'

Mary ran to the window. ' 'Tis true!' she gasped. 'The mourners bear the coffin into the courtyard and a great crowd gathers. Yes, they carry him into the back room of the inn!'

'For laying out,' Hind explained. 'He's to be buried tomorrow in St George's churchyard.'

The information caused a clamour among the drinkers. Only Wild sat unmoved, the dark cloud over his head gathering. 'Sit!' he told Hind.

The York man's legs folded under him and he sank into a seat opposite Wild, dropping his bag to the floor.

'You have brought the letter?' Wild asked, glancing at the bag.

'Yes,' Hind replied.

'Good. And the money and the plate?'

'A great deal of it,' Hind replied, his large hands trembling as he fumbled with the buckle that fastened his bag.

'And with the rest of the money you have paid artists to amend the hallmarks on the silverware?' Wild laid down his cards and for the first time looked directly at the man who acted as his main fence in the city of York, and throughout that vast county.

'Not yet,' Hind admitted. It was sweat now, not rain, that trickled down his temples.

Wild thumped the table and the pewter pots jumped and rattled. The uproar caused by the arrival of Turpin's corpse died down. All eyes were turned on Wild and Hind.

'You think to cheat me and keep money back!' Wild exclaimed, seizing Hind by the throat.

Time for me to sneak out, I judged, for 'never linger where trouble brews' is my motto. And what better diversion than to slip next door, into the room where the mourners worked?

I closed the door on the brawl, finding that the mourners had lifted Turpin out of the coffin and laid him on a plain board, then departed, probably to slake their thirst. The room was small – scarcely large enough to contain the coffin and the corpse – with lime-washed walls, a second door, a shuttered window and a single candle standing on the sill.

There's nothing like the stillness given off by a dead man. A pale, waxy stillness – an absence, you would say. 'Tis the spirit that has departed, and may be hovering above us, looking down on our actions, for all I know. And yet often there's an unnerving notion that your man isn't dead, that he may spring up like O'Neill and stop your own heart dead with fright.

I shuddered and forced my attention on to Turpin's green frock-coat. Its buttons were of brass, with a horse's head design. The new pumps were of soft Spanish leather. I idly considered their value.

'Damn your eyes for thinking of thieving from a dead man!' The chief mourner – an old man grown fat on roast beef and ale, whose waistcoat buttons strained to contain his great belly – had returned, squeezing himself into the room and correctly reading my intention. 'Charley Feather, you'd best make yourself scarce, or I'll call the magistrate's men down on you.' I'm known in these parts, you see.

I backed off, hands up in surrender, out of the door through which I'd entered and straight into what can only be called a desperate situation.

Wild no longer had his hands around Hind's neck, but instead had a gleaming knife at his throat, which showed that events had moved on somewhat and Wild meant business.

Other customers in the tavern had taken exception to the production of the knife and flown to the aid of the local man, to which O'Neill and Delamere had in turn objected and begun throwing Hind's helpers to the floor and giving them a severe beating.

Mary too had played her part by seizing the hair of the landlord's wife and demanding that the man did not make good his threat to call for the magistrate.

What I, Charley Feather, would give to be out of here, with a clean bed and a quiet pillow to lay my head upon, I lamented to myself.

Wild, when roused, is frightening to behold. Twice the size of Hind, and three times as strong, he backed the puny silversmith against a wall, pressing the blade to his Adam's apple.

'Put down the knife, or by God I will have you thrown in gaol!' Sykes called from behind a keg of beer.

His wife squealed and screamed in the grip of Mary Brazier.

'You are already in my debt to the tune of three hundred guineas!' Wild cried, thumping Hind back against the wall.

I ducked as a wooden stool whizzed by my head, launched by the man O'Neill had attacked. Frenchy picked up his latest assailant and hurled him clean through the window.

And who can say that the blow Wild struck with his knife was deliberate? Perhaps he did not intend to fall upon poor Hind, but was pushed from behind. The brawl was confused enough, and involved twenty men. In any case, the silversmith slid to the floor with a low groan and a gush of blood from the wound in his throat.

'Come!' Mary grabbed me by the arm. 'Charley, the game is up. You must make a run for it!'

But the sight of blood makes me faint; I lose power over my limbs.

Mary shook me from my torpor. 'Charley, the rogue is dead. Sykes has called for the magistrate's men!'

I took a deep breath and turned away from Hind lying in a pool of blood. Three strong Yorkshiremen held Wild with his arms pinned behind his back.

O'Neill and Delamere still scrapped and brawled with their opponents.

'We will get out of here!' Mary promised. 'We have been in worse scrapes by far. Now, Charley, run!'

So saying, she shoved me through the small door into the room where the corpse of the late Richard Turpin lay in cold, calm splendour.

Save for the body, the room was empty. The candle by the window was almost spent, its wick starting to smoke, the flame to gutter.

No more thoughts now for the pumps of Spanish leather, though the horse-head buttons still gave me pause for thought, until I heard the heavy, running step of the magistrate's men enter the courtyard, and then my mind was set once again on escape.

I began to wrench and shove at the window shutter, bolted from the outside. I was in luck, for a rusty hinge gave way and the board fell to the ground with a clatter. But the fight had spilled out into the cobbled courtyard, and I must bide my time.

I glanced round at Turpin, musing that I had not thought to follow him so quick to the gallows when I watched him swing not three hours earlier. My breath came short, but I felt a swift, sharp determination that Charley Feather would not dance that same jig.

I heard shouts, some screams, then two shots from a pistol which soon cleared onlookers from the scene.

The courtyard emptied, as if by magic. People ran in all directions. Now was my chance. I climbed onto the window sill, knocking the candle to the floor. Glancing back, I saw the inner door fly open and Mary standing there, until two men seized her and a third came towards me. Quickly, I slipped my skinny frame through the narrow casement, felt a hand try to lay hold of my leg, then heard a voice cry, 'The gap is too narrow to follow, confound it!'

Then I was in the empty courtyard; another pistol was fired. I was under the archway, past the sign of the Blue Boar swinging in the wind, on to Castlegate. I passed three armed men running towards the inn, darted down an alleyway, and came out on a broad, paved street which I knew would lead me all the way to Tadcaster and freedom.

But of Wild, O'Neill, Delamere and Mary I knew nothing and feared the worst.

Two

In which I find a poor billet for the night, reflect on my murky past and ponder my uncertain future.

Now this had unsettled my plans somewhat.

I never expected to be fleeing through the narrow streets of York late on a Saturday afternoon, with the wind whistling around my ears, nor to see two men die in one day; for I'm certain that Jasper Hind has breathed his last, there on the floor of the Blue Boar Inn.

I don't like surprises. I like to measure my days. I am up when the cock crows, making a hearty breakfast at a friendly inn or farmhouse, fetching my horse from the ostler and taking to the road with Frenchy, Mary and O'Neill.

One or two small pieces of business later, during which no one is harmed, God willing, and our saddlebags are stuffed with plunder, we retire to a safe house, to wile away a pleasant evening playing cards.

No unexpected encounters with magistrates' men or duels with travellers foolish enough to resist Delamere's charming manner of parting them from their possessions. For me, that is a good day, and ones such as today amount to nothing short of disaster.

I was pausing for breath under the overhanging roof of a butcher's shop, looking over my shoulder and wondering what best to do, when a woman rushed out from indoors and accosted me.

'Here, boy, you will catch me a rat!' she demands, dragging me into the shop. Whole pigs hang from hooks, heads hacked off, but complete with tails and trotters. Sides of beef lie stacked on a great wooden block.

'I will do no such thing!' I protest, escaping from her clutches. 'I am no rat-catcher, mistress!'

'Oh ho!' she replies, lifting her skirts and giving me a hefty kick. 'I see now your coat is too good and the feather in your hat too grand. And yet you lack a good meal and are skinny enough, so crawl under that bench and catch me the rat!'

I don't argue further, not with the great, cruel meat hooks dangling from the rail, and the cleaver close at hand. So crawl I do.

The cornered rat peers at me with beady eyes, its pouchy body pressed against the wall. As I make as if to grab the creature, it shoots out into the open where Mistress Butcher waits with the cleaver. One whack and the rat is no more.

I emerge, my hat at a crooked angle, step over the rat and bolt.

' 'Tis Charley Feather!' a neighbour cries. 'There is a brawl at the Blue Boar. A man's throat is cut, Charley's confederates are taken!'

And this set off a fresh pursuit, in which I ducked down more alleyways, jumped ditches and open sewers, scattered sheep from their market pen and made good to vanish into a cellar during the uproar. I waited there an hour or two until the busybodies and bounty hunters drifted away.

I shook my head and sighed; I gritted my teeth and vowed to abandon this life. *I'll find myself a new guardian*, I promised. *One who will not be thrown into gaol, like Jem Rowden and Moll Mountjoy, or shipped off to the colonies, like Bess Ainsworth.* As you see, I've had my share of guardians, but no memory of either father or mother.

Before Mary, Bess was my last guardian. Convicted of picking pockets, she was sent from Southwark to Southampton to be shipped off to the New World – lucky to escape the noose, as the judge told her plainly.

I was to sail with her to America, but jumped ship at the last minute and waved goodbye to my latest 'mother', for I preferred not to sail across the wide ocean to a land full of savages and cut-throats.

Bess shed no tears at my departure and hastily wished

me luck. 'You have a good head on young shoulders, Charley,' said she. 'May you rise above this low life and find happiness at last.'

I returned to the streets of London and discovered not happiness, but countless thousands – a whole tide of children such as I, orphaned and cut adrift. There were not enough pockets to pick nor rotten fruit to lift out of the gutter to feed us all, and so I lay starving on the wharf side, which is where Mary discovered me and nursed me back to health.

And that was when I decided upon continuing the great secret, which I keep to this day.

Up out of the cellar and dusting myself down, I started back on the open road, hoping this time to remain unaccosted, even considering taking off my feathered hat to keep myself from notice, until I remembered that my red curls were enough to invite curiosity and so kept my hat clamped to my head.

By now, evening was fast approaching and the light fading from a leaden sky. I had the Knavesmire within view on my left and could see the course laid out for the horses, where men gambled on a winner and riders flayed their flagging mounts to within an inch of their lives.

Beyond the green concourse, further west, the countryside opened out into fields of wheat and barley.

It was at one of these farms that Wild and the rest of us had stabled our horses the night before, and it was to this place that I was now headed. With luck, I could creep into the barn, secure my own mount and ride away into the night without a by-your-leave.

But the sight of the Three-legged Mare, tall and dark against the sky, made me shudder afresh, and I grew tired. My legs ached, my belly was tight with fear. Besides, if I rode now, it would be through the thick night, and I was no Dick Turpin to ride the York to London road at midnight, and my horse was no Black Bess.

No – as I approached the farm, I formed another notion, which was to sneak into the barn where the horses were kept, climb unseen into the hayloft and there spend as peaceful a night as I could.

I achieved this without fuss, though the approach was flat and the land offered scant concealment except that of thick hedgerows and deep ditches. So I arrived at the barn scratched and muddy, scarcely recognisable as the jaunty youth who had sallied forth twenty-four hours earlier.

My grey mare, Guinevere, knew me, though. She raised her head from the manger and cocked an ear. I patted her nose and passed by. 'Eat your fill,' I whispered, 'for tomorrow we must ride.'

Then I forced my weary legs up the ladder into the loft and lay down in the sweet-smelling hay.

* * *

I dreamed that night of sailing through clear, blue waves under a brilliant sky. I climbed the main mast and looked out towards the New World, where I would meet Bess Ainsworth and live with her on a prairie where she raised cattle and went to church on a Sunday. For Bess did not pick pockets out of free choice, but to fill her belly and that of the infant she'd adopted. I missed Bess sorely after I jumped ship, and often thought that America might not have proved the bad land I had feared.

In my dream my ship forged westwards through the waves. I sat in the crow's nest and my heart soared with the gulls overhead.

'Charley, by God!' A voice broke into my slumber. 'Move over, let a man lie down and rest!'

I twisted and sat bolt upright, feeling for the knife in the waistband of my breeches.

'Charley, 'tis me, Delamere!' the voice continued in the dark.

And then I recognised the French tones and breathed again. 'You were not taken?' I whispered.

'No. But the rest were.' Frenchy, as Mary had christened him, made a hollow in the hay to conceal the items he carried, then crouched beside me.

'All of them?'

'Aye. And Jasper Hind is dead. Wild is taken for murder.'

The words hammered at my chest. 'Mary is taken?' I asked. For Wild and O'Neill I cared nothing.

Delamere nodded, then waited until his breathing grew even. 'The crowd turned against us and held us until the magistrate's men came. Wild and O'Neill fired their pistols and injured three, including the landlord, Sykes. His wife fell down in a dead faint, and while they tended her, I broke away and made good my escape.'

I listened without interruption, then asked where Mary and the others were held.

'At York Castle. 'Tis an infamous arrest. There will be a flock of people to see Wild, and they will buy him drink and carouse with him. Wild will not suffer as other prisoners do.'

'Aye, until they hang him by the neck until he is dead,' I whispered, after which, Delamere said nothing.

We each sat lost in thought a while. I grieved for poor Mary – who I judged to be under O'Neill's influence – who had cared for many orphan children, and who, like Bess, would not be a thief unless necessity had dictated it. And I recalled how her hand had flown to her pretty neck when I told her the tale of Turpin's hanging.

'You and I must make our way together,' Delamere said at last.

Aye, at least to London, I agreed silently. I nodded at him and felt him clap his arm around my shoulder.

'Come, Charley, we will prosper!'

'We will,' I agreed.

'Take heart. We are rid of Thomas Wild.'

'Hush!' I warned.

'Charley, he is in the condemned man's cell. They will hang him without delay.'

'We are not free of him until the noose is tightened,' I warned. For myself, I was more glad to be rid of Patrick O'Neill. I've seen him hit out at Mary many a time, and have avoided his heavy fist myself.

But Frenchy lay back in the hay, his arms behind his head. I caught his handsome profile in a shaft of moonlight that fell through a gap in the stable roof.

Delamere claims noble French blood, and his taste in fine lace and good brandy makes me half believe him. But they say he drank and gambled his way out of a fortune, stole gold plate from a duke to pay off his debts and was caught. In Paris they don't hang a man from a rope, but chop his head clean off.

'Tis also said that Delamere fled the guillotine on a ship to England and fell in with one of Wild's gangs in Holborn. Wild likes the company of men of manners and good taste. He took to Delamere and said he meant to make him head of one of his gangs. From there, it was only a short step to the Great North Road and the life of a highwayman.

I suspect that O'Neill resisted coming under the

Frenchman, saying he could not be trusted, but Wild knew that the guillotine hung over Delamere's head back in France and this gave him power over him. Besides, Frenchy can charm the gold sovereigns out of a traveller's pocket with his *s'il vous plait*s and *merci*s. The ladies swoon as he springs from the saddle and falls onto his knee to kiss their hands before he swipes the rubies from their necks and diamonds from their fingers.

Do *I* trust him as I lie there beside him? Am I won over by the handsome profile and the friendly arm around my shoulder?

'Come, lad!' he says to me, moonlight playing on his clean-shaven face, his foreign voice sliding up and down the scale. 'This is a new beginning for us. I will teach you the manners of a French count; we will win our ways into the hearts of the great ladies of England!'

His final words come close to the heart of my dilemma, though I will not confess it to Delamere. It presses hard on me now, though I've taken pains to avoid thinking of it since Mary first found me dressed in borrowed rags. I had neither shoes nor a coat to protect me – only a torn shirt and worn-out breeches.

'What is your name?' Mary had asked when she took me up and carried me home.

'Charley,' I whispered in a swoon from hunger.

'This is Charley,' she announced to the rest of her brood, when she laid me near the embers in the hearth, preparing to go out once more. 'Give the lad broth and bread, for he is starving and I could not leave him to die.'

My common name for as long as I have been able to speak and understand is Charley. But listen well – my full name is Charlotte Sharpe, given, I suppose, by my mother, for it was the name written on a slip of paper and pinned to the rough shawl wrapped around me when Jem Rowden's lurcher dog sniffed me out under the church porch in Cheapside, and I was then a baby not six months old.

'What do you say, Charley?' Frenchy insisted. 'Will you learn to dance a gavotte and charm the ladies? Will you follow in the footsteps of your friend, the great Claude Delamere?'

Three

The question of trust is quickly resolved. We leave
York and head south. Delamere demonstrates his
skill on the highway, then burdens me with a
great secret of his own.

No one is what they seem. I've seen bold gentlemen
bristling with silver pistols desert their ladies in a flash
and run to hide in the bushes when faced with the
masked figure of a highwayman. And many high and
mighty ladies are more than willing to sacrifice their
honour to a French thief, believe me.

What am I thinking! Am I out of my wits to dream of
trusting Frenchy and revealing my sex? How long would
his gallantry stretch, I wondered, once he knew he was
in the company, of not Charley but of Charlotte Feather.

The moment of weakness passed. 'I will learn to dance
and deceive,' I consented gruffly.

'Hah!' Frenchy laughed. 'Good lad!' he said, pulling
his greatcoat about him and settling down to sleep.

* * *

The 'good lad' and the Frenchman set off before dawn the next morning – a Sunday, and so few were on the road to keep us company. Our horses were rested and well fed, and we left the three mounts belonging to Wild, O'Neill and Mary with the farmer, Samuel Ward, who was about early and swore not to set the magistrate's men on our trail. The horses were sound and amounted in value to twenty guineas – more than enough to silence Ward, we hoped.

I rode my grey mare and Delamere took to the road on a tall bay hunter named Duc D'Orleans, or Duke for short.

We had not travelled two miles along the grey, deserted track before we reached a crossroads overhung by a broad oak upon whose gnarled trunk had been freshly posted an account of 'The Trial of the Notorious Highwayman, Richard Turpin, and His Behaviour at the Place of Execution.'

Recognising the letters comprising Turpin's name, Delamere reined his horse to a halt.

'Read it to me,' he commanded. 'This damned, cramped English hand is impossible to decipher.'

I did as I was bid, it being Bess who had taught me my letters, in the hope, no doubt, that it would assist me on my road towards happiness. ' "At York Assizes on the twenty-second day of March, 1739, before Hon. Sir William Chapple . . ." ' I began.

'No, no – the part about the execution,' Frenchy interrupted.

I cast my eye down the bill. ' "Wherein Turpin acknowledged himself guilty of the crimes of which he stood accused and gave a particular account of several more robberies which he had committed." '

Delamere tutted impatiently. 'I would not confess! They would have to tear my tongue out first.'

'I'm hungry,' I complained, sick of reading about Turpin, and turning Guinevere towards Tadcaster and a breakfast of ham and bread at the King's Arms.

'Whoa!' Frenchy trotted up alongside. 'Not so fast, Charley.' (Spoken by him as 'Shar-lee', which brings a smile to my lips.) 'How will you reward the innkeeper?'

I had no money, I acknowledged, and kept to myself for the time being the pretty gold locket I had about my person.

So Delamere winked and patted his saddlebag. 'I will pay.' He grinned, leading the way at a full gallop through a stream, taking a short cut across the fields into town.

We tethered the horses by the riverbank, at the foot of an old stone bridge next to a forge. I took the precaution of removing my tell-tale hat and secreting it under my saddle. Frenchy tossed a copper coin at the blacksmith's lad.

'Look out for these beasts,' he ordered, then went

swaggering off on to the high street, to the consternation of a churchgoing family alighting from a closed carriage onto the narrow pavement.

The family consisted of mother, father, three daughters and a son. Delamere strode through them as if parting the Red Sea.

'Oh, Walter!' the woman gasped. 'I am almost bowled off my feet.'

The husband glared at Frenchy, who however stared him down with ease.

'Forgive me, *madame*.' Frenchy remembered his manners and bowed low. 'Please – walk with me. Take my arm, I will lead you across the road to your church!'

Call it a sort of magic, but the buttoned-up woman in her Sunday gown forgot her distress and melted before him. 'You are a Frenchman?' she inquired.

'*Oui, madame*.' He nodded, standing to attention and offering her his arm.

She smiled and sighed, took the arm and floated across the muddy street while her husband rounded up their offspring. Then she thanked him as he bowed even lower than before and waved her through the church gate.

'Food!' I reminded Frenchy wearily when he saw fit to return.

So we went into the inn, sat down at table and ate a good breakfast, with me speaking for us both since

Frenchy feared recognition after his encounter on the street.

His silence gave us plenty of opportunity to overhear talk between the landlord and the town barber who had arrived at the inn to shave mine host.

At first, the conversation was all about the hanging – how Turpin had died game and his followers had wept. I chewed hard on my ham and kept my eyes fixed on the table. *Turpin. Always Turpin and his date with death.*

Then the landlord and barber turned to the brawl at the Blue Boar.

'The rogue, Wild, slit the throat of his own man,' the barber reported, sharpening his razor on a strap. 'Jasper Hind bled to death for all to see.'

I chewed on but found I couldn't swallow the meat. Frenchy, with his back to the two men, winked at me. But he was tense, nonetheless.

'The villain is safe in the county gaol,' the landlord reported, tilting his head back and falling silent at the scrape of the razor over his skin.

'Aye, along with two members of his gang.' The barber went about his business with a steady hand. 'Though two others escaped, they say. A cunning Frenchman and a lad, who must be racing hell for leather for London by now, if they know what's good for them.'

'I know nothing of that,' the landlord grunted. 'But I breathe easier now that Turpin and Wild are both in irons.'

Turning to the window and catching sight of my own reflection, I was startled by the appearance of my hatless head and of the curls sprouting from my scalp. The clustering locks gave my face an unwanted softness and roundness, which together with the smoothness of my cheeks, could give rise to suspicion.

So I stood up and made an excuse to Frenchy, passing close to the barber and lightly lifting a pair of scissors from his apron pocket without his notice. I escaped outside, ducked across the street into the church, waiting awhile on a back pew until the service ended and the congregation filed out. Then I looked around me until I found the silver communion dish. Propping it against the back of a pew, I crouched down to view my peculiar reflection.

I saw a distorted face surrounded by a halo of red curls and so, taking the scissors, I snipped them off a handful at a time until my whole head was almost bare. The curls lay scattered on the pew and the floor like the downy under-feathers of a golden goose.

I nodded at my new cropped image in the silver dish, reckoned up the value of the plate, thought better of it and returned it to its shelf in the vestry. Then I ran back to the inn.

'By God, Shar-lee!' Frenchy exclaimed when he saw my new trim.

The barber had finished his task and sat drinking with the landlord. Both men looked across sharply, hearing his foreign voice for the first time.

'Pay up and leave!' I hissed at Frenchy, seeing that we had outstayed our welcome. 'Come!'

No sooner said than Frenchy slapped down some coins and we were gone.

Back at the foot of the bridge, however, all was not well. There was Guinevere, securely tethered, her head hanging and sighing for our return, but where was Duke?

In a frenzy, Delamere rushed into the blacksmith's shop and accosted the boy he had set to keep watch over his horse. He seized him by the scruff of his neck, dangling him in the air as if attempting to shake an explanation from him.

'Numbskull!' he exclaimed. 'How came my horse to wander off? There are items in that saddlebag worth a king's ransom!'

But then the smith himself strode across the forge, red-hot iron in hand. The fellow was tall and in his prime, with a short, bull-like neck and forearms as thick as my waist. Seeing this hulk out of the corner of his eye, Frenchy dropped the lad and took a hasty leave.

'My horse!' he complained, striding up and down the wharf side. 'What can a man do without his horse!'

And his saddlebag, which was not his but Hind's, containing items worth a king's ransom, I thought. This had come as interesting news to me.

However, Duke had not gone far, and we discovered him barely a hundred paces away, on a patch of grass beside a great water wheel that drove the engine of a tall flour mill.

'Thank God!' Frenchy cried, seizing the reins and dragging the creature away.

Then he was up and in the saddle, turning him around, glad to leave the town of Tadcaster behind and continue our flight towards the south.

Early April brings blossom to the blackthorn and the faint promise of spring. There is green in the hedgerows, though the limbs of the tall trees are bare. 'Tis a good season for the traveller, for the ground is unfrozen, but not yet mired underfoot.

'We must push on!' Delamere cried, his coat flying behind him as Duke galloped through the Yorkshire countryside.

I crouched low in the saddle and bade Guinevere keep up, thinking all the while of what to do now that Wild was off the scene and all his gangs leaderless.

My choices were narrow. Either I stuck with Frenchy

and took my chance with him, or I cut loose once we had reached London and made my own way in that crowded, cruel city. With Delamere, I would be sure of protection and guidance. We would swagger around town, telling thrilling tales of our exploits. Men would offer us shelter and women would flock to us. When necessity drove us, we would venture back on to the highway.

However, another picture formed in my mind as we galloped on. It was of me casting off my disguise and donning a petticoat, turning myself into a maidservant for hire in the great households, tearing myself free from the life I had led until now. A poor servant who would rise before dawn to clean grates and carry chamberpots, whose fingers would be worked to the bone in kitchens and cellars, whose face would never see the light of day, whose stomach would be fed scraps left over by the master's dogs.

I shook my head at this and took note of the brown, ploughed fields showing shoots of green, of sparrows building their nests, and the brow of the hill ahead.

Over this brow we came upon another town which I knew to be Wetherby. Frenchy slowed to a trot and told me that we would skirt the dwellings and pass on without stopping, though our horses were blowing hard.

'Then we must rest under this cliff before we go on,' I told him.

He consented, staying in the saddle, but drawing off the road into the shelter of a copse of hazels growing in the lea of a rocky outcrop.

We had been there five minutes, and poor Guinevere was breathing more easily, when a chance arose that Delamere could not resist. We heard horses approach along a quiet bridleway to our left and soon two ladies appeared, riding fine grey hunters, out for a leisurely Sunday stroll.

'Oho!' says Frenchy, judging by the quality of the mounts that they were ladies of some wealth. He tucks himself further out of sight.

The ladies chatter about this and that.

'I am not a piece of property for my father to hand about the market-place,' says one proudly. 'He may be the richest wool merchant in the county, but when it comes to marriage, I will do the choosing!'

'Yes,' says the other quietly.

'Aha!' murmurs Frenchy.

The proud one holds her head high under a blue velvet riding hat adorned with a great plume of dyed feathers. 'Joseph Rose does not suit me,' she continues.

'But he bids high,' the quiet one remarks. 'His father is a baronet and owns half the land in Derbyshire.'

Frenchy's grey eyes glitter. Then he bursts forth from the copse and levels a pistol at the fine lady's head. 'Forgive me, *mesdemoiselles!*' he cries. 'For I must part you from whatever you have of value about your persons!'

The fine lady shrieks and commences with a great fuss, but her companion looks Frenchy in the eye. 'Sir, you have chosen poorly,' she tells him. 'For I am a clergyman's daughter and carry nothing of value.'

I see from her plain dress and demure manner that this is true.

Frenchy concurs, waves her aside and tells me to draw my knife. 'Keep the little mouse quiet,' he orders.

I do as I am told and point my blade at the clergyman's daughter, who is calm and disdainful throughout.

Now Delamere's attention is all on the shrieking lady. '*Mademoiselle*,' he says, 'I will not harm you. Calm yourself.'

His suave, smooth tone halts the noise. 'I have no money about me,' says the stuttering, sobbing victim.

'Ah, but you must part with that pretty ring on your finger, and that brooch of gold on your breast,' Frenchy cajoles, as if begging a dance at a county ball. 'Come, my lady, they are but trinkets.'

'Make no move!' I warn the clergyman's plain daughter, who makes as if to rein her horse to one side and gallop away.

'A fine lady such as you must own a huge hoard of

jewels, given by a whole host of admirers,' Frenchy flatters the other.

And the lady simpers and begins to smile a little. ' 'Twas Joseph Rose who gave me this sapphire ring,' she confesses.

'Then you will not be sorry to let it go,' Frenchy declares, riding close to her, leaning out and asking for her dainty hand, which she gives willingly, as if under a spell. Frenchy twists the ring from her finger, one set about with emeralds and pearls, and tosses it in the air, where it sparkles, before slipping it into his deep pocket. 'And now the brooch,' he beseeches.

The lady pouts. ' 'Tis my mother's,' she protests.

'A pretty thing,' he tells her. 'But your mother will be glad of your safe return and when you tell her of the ordeal you have undergone, she will not care for the gems you have lost.'

And so the fine lady unpins the brooch and hands it over.

Frenchy receives it then lands a light kiss on her white hand. 'Tell your father that he values you too lightly.'

'How so?' comes the simpering response.

My plain vicar's daughter curls her lip in scorn.

'In future he must not let you ride in the country alone with Mistress Mouse. You need a strong fellow by your side to protect you.'

'Aye, and this a Sunday morning too!' says my severe lady with a loud tut, meaning that it is the Lord's day.

Frenchy laughs and bows to them both. We rein in our horses and prepare to depart. '*Au revoir!*' he tells them, lifting his hat with a flourish. 'You have lightened our journey, *mesdemoiselles*!'

The first lady blushes under her blue hat. '*Au revoir,*' she returns breathily.

And then we are gone, Frenchy and me, fixing our weapons into our belts, whirling Duke and Guinevere away from the place of our meeting, galloping off into the distance.

'Perfect!' Delamere cries above the wind. 'Charley, we will prosper, you and I!'

That evening, after a hard day's riding, we crossed the border into the county of Derbyshire and made our way to a small village and the safe house of one Samuel Nott.

The house was low and built of stone, tucked away behind a sheep fold on the edge of the village. Nott himself offers good food and ale and a warm, clean bed without prying into a man's business. He has but one arm, the other having been lost in an accident when he was a youth, though I don't know in what manner this came about.

We and our horses were housed well and left to ourselves beside a great fire. Our beds were of straw and laid out on the floor, in the space which Nott uses to brew strong ale out of hops and barley.

'I am for bed!' I told Delamere as the logs on the fire shifted and settled. My legs ached after the long ride and my mind still whirled from the narrowness of our escape from York.

My companion did not answer, busy as he was with a sealed envelope which he had taken out from his precious saddlebag. 'The writing of this address be damned!' he muttered.

I lay down on my mattress, staring into the embers, watching the red light flicker across the rough wall.

Frenchy shook his head. 'The letters are damnably crooked. I cannot make them out.'

To me, from a distance and in the dim firelight, it looked an even and plain enough hand. I yawned and turned my face away, listening to Frenchy hum and haw.

'Shar-lee, I say this is a horrible English scribble and I cannot make it out! You must read it for me.'

'Tomorrow will be time enough.' I sighed.

'Ah, but you do not understand.'

I felt Delamere's hand on my shoulder and was forced to roll back towards him. 'What don't I understand?' I asked wearily.

'I have come by this letter and I cannot make out to whom it should be delivered.'

'You have stolen it,' I interpreted plainly.

'Aye, and I believe it to be a valuable paper, Charley.'

'How so?' I felt a tingle of interest begin at the base of my neck and travel down my spine.

Frenchy shook his head. 'It was at the Blue Boar. You recall, Wild remarked upon a certain paper . . .'

'*This* same paper!' Lunging forward, I tried to wrest it from Frenchy's grasp.

He whisked it out of reach. 'Yes, this paper.'

'Give it to me!' I cried. He refused, so then I looked around for the saddlebag that Hind had brought to the inn, which had begun the quarrel with Wild. Frenchy himself had said that it contained a king's ransom and now I was determined to unearth the treasure. I soon found it under Frenchy's mattress, held it up high and shook the contents onto the floor.

Out dropped watches and chains, snuff-boxes and bejewelled ivory fans. Over the stone flags rolled gold coins; banknotes fluttered through the air.

Frenchy sat back and studied my amazement. 'Well?' he asked.

'This is Hind's bag, intended for Wild! It contains what Hind owed him.'

Frenchy nodded.

'You stole it from the man who controls all the thieves

and murderers of London!' My voice was high and breathless. I could not believe my eyes.

'I did,' Frenchy agreed with a smile. 'For what good is it to Thomas Wild at the end of a hangman's rope?'

Four

*In which my companion fondly believes himself to be
Fortune's darling, time passes and we come across a
particular friend in familiar circumstances.*

Delamere's news made my heart hammer against my
ribs. 'You have taken a mighty risk by stealing this bag!'
I declared. 'Wild is feared up and down the country.
None dare cross him.'

Delamere smiled. 'The walls of York County Gaol
are thick. The justices will try Thomas Wild and hang
him before the week is out.'

I shook my head, picturing reasons for a lengthier
imprisonment. 'They may take time to gather
witnesses. 'Tis not a swift business. Besides, Wild's
men are everywhere, and when they hear of this
theft it will not be safe for us to set foot on the
street.'

'Who will stay loyal to Wild?' Frenchy scoffed. 'Not
William Plommer, nor Thomas Heath, for I know they
abhor the villain. Come, Charley, name me one who

will remain under Wild's thumb, now that he is taken, or one who will blame me for my actions.'

I frowned and began to pace the small room.

'Charley!' Frenchy appealed, airily rising above my fears. 'Would you have walked away from such a prize? Why, Hind's bag lay under the table unnoticed. Should I have left it for some other villain to seize? No! There it lay with no one to own it, and so I carried it off!'

Slowly, I nodded. 'Were you seen?' I asked.

'I slipped away like a shadow,' Frenchy assured me. 'Men with broken heads lay here and there, the women were wailing, Wild and O'Neill were cursing as the magistrate's men dragged them away. No one noticed me pick up the bag and leave.'

'Very well.' I found myself partly won over, mistakenly, as you will see.

'Why so sober and severe?' Frenchy cajoled, pinching my cheek until he forced a smile. 'You are the companion of Claude Delamere, he who escaped Madame Guillotine and who has never set eyes on the inside of a prison cell. Why, good fortune accompanies my every step!'

I looked at him in his cambric shirt with cuffs of finest lace, with his dark hair curling about his cheeks and his eyes that were never still, but danced and sparkled with life.

'Charley, Thomas Wild has a date with death,' he

reminded me. He took up the letter that had begun our argument and carefully secreted it inside his shirt. Then he began to sort through the items of jewellery and plate. 'Lady Luck is with us. Take this diamond pin – see how it shines!'

I have seen it before – how some men believe themselves untouchable, the very feather in Fortune's cap. And I knew Delamere was of that kind. But 'tis like saying a man may not catch the plague, when the evidence is before our eyes that all may fall victim, be he beggar in the stinking gutter or high and mighty justice of the peace.

The diamond glittered in the dim firelight. ' 'Tis pretty,' I confessed, leaving Frenchy to pore over the spoils while I lay down my head and tried to sleep.

Time, however, settled my fears.

The following day broke clear and bright and so we headed south apace.

'God be praised for a stout horse and fair going underfoot!' Delamere would shout at full gallop. Or, 'We have the luck of the devil, Charley, and a following wind to aid us!'

I couldn't help but smile, and so grew more hopeful with the passing days.

My spirits were up and blood coursed lustily through

my veins when it came to Wednesday, which was another day of spring sunshine, broken only by one light shower sometime after noon.

We had dried out and found an inn for the night, near to the market town named Five Oaks in Nottinghamshire, when my companion took a fancy to a night-time escapade.

'What do you say to an adventure?' he asked me as I sat with my feet on the table in front of the landlord's blazing fire.

I yawned and feigned tiredness. 'I have had adventure enough this past week.'

But Frenchy tutted and cursed me for being idle and worse. 'Are you a coward, Charley? Where is your spirit, lad?'

So I had to jump up and ride, for no man may call me 'coward'.

'I heard talk of a coach coming in from the south at midnight,' Frenchy informed me. 'The ostlers at the Cross Keys grumbled at the late hour and the proud ways of Lady Georgiana Bedford, whose coach it is.'

'This must be the Lady Georgiana whose husband, Sir Henry Bedford, commanded a regiment in the Spanish Wars,' I reflected, watching light clouds scud across the crescent moon. I pride myself on knowing the business of gentry throughout the land. 'Sir Henry owns an estate of some two thousand acres in the county of Norfolk.'

This was music to Frenchy's ears. He spurred Duke on towards the crossroads he had chosen for our ambush, and when we reached the spot, he sought the cover of five broad oaks, whence, no doubt, the town took its name, and where the shade was darkest and the thick trunks and low branches would hide us.

'Stand!' a deep voice cried as we urged our horses under the trees.

Guinevere reared onto her hind legs and staggered backwards, almost unseating me.

Delamere pulled out his pistol, which glinted in the moonlight. 'Who tells us to stand?' he yelled back.

Three figures emerged on horseback, each brandishing a weapon, faces concealed by broad-brimmed hats worn low.

'Who needs to know?' came the challenge. The three highwaymen surrounded us, jostling Frenchy and me into the deep shadow cast by the oaks.

'By God!' Frenchy muttered. 'We have been beaten to it!'

'Answer!' came the gruff command.

So, with a laugh, Frenchy doffed his hat. 'You speak to Claude Delamere and young Charley Feather. We are sorry to stand in your way, gentlemen. 'Tis only that we sought a small diversion and a little profit on our journey to London.'

With this, the hats of our rivals came off and we gave friendly greetings to gruff Tom Cox and Jack Bird, together with my old acquaintance, Robert Major.

Tom Cox is a Midlands man who rarely ventures out of his way due to a comely wife and a liking for home comforts. Jack Bird, a man of three score years, follows where Tom leads. Robert, of whom more later, has also joined the gang.

' 'Tis an unlucky night for you, Frenchy,' Cox began, clasping my companion by the hand. 'We had set our minds on the Bedford coach and laid plans before you came upon the scene.'

Frenchy nodded. 'It would be a pity for us to return empty-handed, Tom. What say you to joining together in this enterprise? Five pairs of hands would make sure of the prize.'

'Three are enough,' Cox grumbled, rubbing his chin. Then, more considerately, 'I hear you and Charley were all but taken at the Blue Boar in York.'

I saw Robert shoot a swift glance at me, so I sat with my shoulders squared, my chin thrust out, devil-may-care.

Then there was no more time for discussion, because old Jack Bird cupped his hand around his ear and declared that a coach was fast approaching and so Cox companionably agreed to share the spoils with Frenchy and me.

I led my horse deep into the shadow, leaning forward in the saddle so that a low branch would conceal me.

'If it ain't little Charley Feather!' Robert Major chuckled, finding a spot for his horse close by.

'Not so much of the "little"!' I retorted. I could feel my heart beat faster at the sound of wheels trundling towards us. This was the moment when fear could seize you by the throat and paralyse you. I warded it off by gritting my teeth and holding my breath.

'Stand and deliver!' Cox and Delamere charged out of the shadows as the heavy coach slowed at the crossroads. They rose high in their stirrups and levelled their weapons at the driver and postillion, while Robert, Jack and I rode out and surrounded the coach.

'Samuel, what in the devil's name is happening?' The head of a very ancient lady with a hooked nose and a long chin rising to meet it appeared at the window. 'Damn you, man, why have we stopped?'

The driver sat silent, like a rabbit caught in the glare of a lamp.

Frenchy rode a step or two nearer. 'You have stopped, my lady, because we wish to lighten your way by parting you from one or two small articles which you carry about your person.'

'Villain!' she screeched. 'You mean to rob me! Samuel,

drive on! Dick, draw your pistol and shoot them through the heart!'

Cox and Bird moved in to ensure that the postillion did no such thing.

'Be calm, my lady,' Delamere soothed. 'I see you wear a brooch in your fine hat and a necklace of rubies around your pretty neck. And perhaps you carry gold sovereigns in your purse.'

' "Be calm"!' the woman screeched, attempting to draw down the blind but prevented in this by Robert. 'I will not be calm, sir! No, I will set my husband's regiment upon you and have you hunted down like vermin.'

'She has not fallen for your charms, Frenchy,' Robert muttered, recovering from a sharp rap on his knuckles from the lady's fan.

'The brooch!' Cox stepped in with a rough, outstretched hand. When Lady Bedford refused, he swept the whole hat from her head and threw it for Bird to catch. 'And now the necklace from around that scrawny neck.'

At which rough aspersion on her feminine charms, she, poor lady, went into a dead faint.

So Robert and I dismounted and took the jewels, along with the embroidered silk purse which lay on the seat beside her. The chink of heavy coins told us that our luck was holding.

And so we bade farewell to Samuel and Dick, assuring them of a good billet ahead of them in Five Oaks, and commiserating with them over the sour nature of their mistress.

'Her nature is nothing to that of the master.' Samuel sighed. 'He is the very devil, you may be sure.'

So Delamere took pity and dipped into the silk purse and slipped them each a gold sovereign, advising them to do no less than desert the insensible Lady Bedford then and there, and to seek their fortunes elsewhere. Whereupon, driver and postillion readily took to their heels and her ladyship awoke from her stupor to find herself abandoned and saw that she must walk the last mile into Five Oaks – in which Delamere spitefully misdirected her down the wrong road while Cox divided the spoils five ways.

'So, Charley, you have had a narrow escape,' Robert began, drawing me to one side. We were on foot, our horses tethered nearby.

' 'Twas nothing,' said I gamely, careful to keep my voice low and steady. 'And you – you have deserted London for the country, I hear.'

'Aye, I grew sick of the London gangs and the dark streets, so I thought to try my hand further north.' Robert settled on the ground, his back against a stout trunk, hands clasped around his knees. Though his face was shadowed, I could see that his eyes were bright and carried a smile about them, as of old.

'What news of Bess?' I inquired. 'Does she prosper in the colonies?'

'She has taken a husband there and he has made her honest,' Robert informed me. 'Think of it, Charley – no more picking pockets for our Bess.'

'Our' Bess calls to mind what I meant to convey before – that Robert Major resided with me in Bess Ainsworth's lodgings, along with five or six other orphans at some time or another, and he, being the eldest, was often charged with our care when Bess had to go about her business.

' 'Tis a miracle,' I replied with a worldly roll of my eyes, but within I was heartily glad at the news. And pleased, too, to come across Robert, for whom I confess warmer feelings than I may show for reasons you may know but he must not. 'There is no maid yet who will make *you* an honest man, is there?' I asked him slyly.

He laughed. 'No, no, I steer clear of the fairer sex, Charley, and I advise you to do the same, you young pup!'

With which he knocked me clean off balance, tumbling me backwards down a small hill, so that I almost shrieked and played the wench. Instead, I scrambled up and boldly cuffed him across the cheek, which led him to wrestle me to the floor and my hat flew off, until I craved mercy and we resumed our talk.

'What has happened to your curls, Charley?' Robert asked, retrieving my hat and fixing it back on my head.

'Gone,' I muttered.

He studied me closely. 'You must put on muscle,' he advised. 'A man could knock you from your horse with a mere breath.'

I pursed my lips and told him that slightness of stature was not to be scoffed at. 'I slip through spaces where no man may follow, I melt into the night.'

'Aye, Charley Feather, 'tis your way!' Robert agreed. 'Light of finger, light of foot.' He seemed about to sigh and reach out for my hand, then prevented himself. 'You must look around you. Trust no one,' he said instead.

Then Cox announced that he was ready to ride home and Frenchy pocketed his share of the sovereigns. Robert and I had to say our farewells.

'There is danger ahead of you, young Charley.' Robert drew me to my feet and hoisted me into the saddle.

I smiled down at him. 'Fear not for me. Look to your own safety, and come again to London when you have breathed enough country air.'

'You intend to go back to London?' he inquired eagerly as Frenchy mounted Duke and let Tom Cox know that we would not return to the Cross Keys, but head south through the night.

I nodded. 'London is like a great maw. It swallows a

man without leaving a crumb behind. Its belly crawls with the likes of Frenchy and me. We will lie low. Then, when Wild is hanged and the gangs are free from his grasp, we will breathe easy and come into the open again.'

Robert shook his head. There was no smile playing about his eyes as he stared up at me. 'You have not heard the latest news?' he murmured.

'Aye, that Wild is taken and lies in York, along with Mary Brazier and Patrick O'Neill? I was there to witness it, remember.'

'No, no. There has been a great change. The Attorney General would have them tried in London, despite the expense to the Crown. On Monday the three prisoners set out with a guard of ten soldiers.'

I shook my head and began to shudder. 'Do not jest, Robert!'

'This is no jest. The news is that Wild, together with Mary and O'Neill, broke free from their guard in a great act of violence. Three of His Majesty's men were killed outright.'

At this, Delamere, who had overheard, jumped from his horse and threw Robert to the ground. He drew his pistol and held it to his temple. 'On your life!' he roared. 'Tell me if this is true!'

My heart lurched when I saw that gun pressing against Robert's head, but I did not cry out.

' 'Tis true!' Robert said calmly.

And Tom Cox stepped in with, 'Wild is free, Frenchy.'

I saw Delamere sag a little, then take a deep breath. He turned to Cox. 'What more?'

Cox left us in no doubt. 'Wild is out of his wits with rage,' he said slowly. 'He has let it be known along the King's highway from York to London, that he is after the heart and lungs of the treacherous villain who stole his property.'

Five

In which the great beast of London stirs. We are pursued on all sides and experience another steep decline in the quality of our lodgings. Containing also a warning to travellers and much to-do concerning the letter.

There was an ache in my limbs from hard riding, so that when I slipped from the saddle just before dawn next morning, my legs were numb and I could not tell if my feet touched the ground. My poor mare, Guinevere, was spent.

'How in the name of the devil did Dick Turpin ride from London to York before the clock turned full circle?' Delamere complained, easing himself from the saddle.

'You must praise his horse, Black Bess, for that,' I reminded him. 'And they say he burst the heart of the brave beast and she fell down dead within sight of the city.' Stroking Guinevere's soft nose and fetching a bag of oats, I promised her that she would not meet the same fate.

'It's damned bad luck that Wild broke free,' Frenchy

muttered, stamping the ground and watching the horizon turn misty grey. The first songs of the blackbird and thrush accompanied our talk.

I stood silent for a while, thinking how I might persuade Wild that I played no part in the theft of Hind's saddlebag. But I grew certain that my own heart and lungs would be torn out before the words had the chance to form in my mouth. And so I resigned myself to staying close by Delamere, whatever the cost.

'I say, Charley, we must look on things in a new light. What must we do now?'

'Cast away the bag?' I suggested. 'Plead ignorance of the business?'

'Hmm.' Frenchy paced up and down the small hillock to our right. 'Would Wild believe us?'

I thought a while, then shook my head. 'If in any doubt, he would have us shot to be on the safe side.'

'So we keep the bag. What else, say you?'

'Flee to another town,' was my next thought. 'We might try Norwich or Oxford, where we are not known.'

'And so we stick out like a sore thumb,' Frenchy commented. 'Who would offer us shelter? How would we escape notice?'

'Then London it must be,' I concluded, though that great, heaving city filled me with dread. I feared William Plommer and Thomas Heath, the main agents for Wild, who had led the gangs since the days of Wild's father,

Jonathan. Though old, they lorded it over every pickpocket and street urchin, as well as blackmailers, thieves and fraudsters of every description.

'There will be many against us,' Frenchy warned. 'News will have travelled like wildfire down the country and across the Thames to Southwark.'

'Better to have thought of this sooner,' I could not refrain from pointing out. I busied myself with Guinevere, taking her into the shelter of a beech tree and offering her water from a roadside trough.

How I found myself suddenly sitting in that horse trough, spluttering and half drowning, I will now describe.

Guinevere bent her head low and was sucking noisily. Delamere was boasting that he would deal with our enemies in a manner that let everyman know that he was greater now than the infamous Thomas Wild, who was a spent force since his arrest and incarceration in York. Then I felt a sudden weight upon my shoulders from above, which thrust me forward into the slimy trough, so that I lost my balance and disappeared under the water next to Guinevere's nose. When I came up for air, I was staring into the grinning face of Robert Major.

'You are a dead man, Charley Feather!' Robert proclaimed, whirling round and aiming his pistol at Frenchy. 'Bang, Mister Delamere!'

I staggered from the trough, dripping from head to foot.

'I took you by surprise, did I not?' Robert cried, lowering his pistol. ' 'Twas easy, let me assure you, to hide in that tree and watch you approach, and if I had not been my own man, but under the employ of Wild, you would be lying cold at my feet!'

'Rogue, you have followed us!' Frenchy stormed.

Robert merely grinned. 'I mean to keep an eye on you and travel with you,' he confided. 'I have had my fill of the country life, Charley. The streets of London draw me back.'

I frowned at him. 'You are playing a sly game,' I muttered, still dripping and displeased. 'Only last night you were set on enjoying Tom Cox's company a while longer. What made you change your mind?'

'Can't one old friend look out for another, Charley. Why, 'twas me who warned you of Wild's escape and told you to be on your guard. And now you repay me with your suspicions.' Laughing, Robert bent to squeeze the tails of my frock-coat.

Then Delamere stepped in to have his say. 'We need no company on the road,' he said plainly. 'Charley and I will reach the city and vanish into its depths. And you, Robert Major, will not follow us.' He spoke seriously, in a low voice, his eye fixed on Robert's.

'Wild's reach is long,' Robert protested. 'I will be

your spy, your informant, your connection with the outside world.'

But Delamere shook his head. 'You are too eager,' he complained.

'I am Charley's friend!' Robert protested. 'We are as close to brothers as may be!'

I smiled weakly and looked down to hide my blushes.

'Nevertheless, we ride alone,' Frenchy decided, taking to the saddle and urging me to do the same. 'If you want to aid Charley further, Robert Major, you will be sure to throw Wild's men off our trail. Say we are headed west for Oxford and intend to lie low in that city until the heat is off.'

Robert grunted as he offered me a leg up. 'I will do what I can,' he agreed, giving my leg a squeeze before he let me go. 'Look around every corner,' he reminded me quietly. 'Trust no one.'

I nodded and reined Guinevere away, following Frenchy down the hill. I glanced once over my shoulder, to see Robert standing by the stone trough, hat in hand, watching us go.

Soon Frenchy slowed his pace. As the sun rose and the day grew warm, he took off his coat and let the fine lace of his collar and cuffs flutter in the breeze, his long dark hair wafting loose. He whistled away the morning down country lanes and across fields which kept us a good distance from the villages and farmhouses. At noon, he stopped, put on his coat and bade me tend the horses by a stream.

'Where will you go?' I asked as he stepped out on foot.

'To a house I know,' he replied guardedly. 'To meet with a man I know.'

A flutter of suspicion soon passed as I watched him climb the bank and head off through a thick copse of beeches. However, I knew Delamere would not long leave Duke and the precious saddlebag slung across the horse's withers. So I climbed a nearby tree and settled on a broad branch, legs astride, back against the trunk, my face turned to the sun, until an hour or more had passed and Delamere returned with a spring in his stride.

'What news?' I asked, sliding to the ground.

For answer, Frenchy patted the pocket of his coat and I heard the heavy chink of coins. By which I understood that he had found his man and traded in Lady Bedford's ruby necklace for a bag full of guineas. And now he looked like the Delamere of old – walking tall, and with a swagger.

'By God, Charley, who says Wild will track us down! We make good progress, do we not?'

I nodded. But I had my eyes peeled. 'Your man nearby will not give us away?' I asked.

Frenchy laughed. 'He is Wild's sworn enemy, once a labourer in the town of Bourne who lost his only son to a bullet from Patrick O'Neill's pistol. His hatred for Wild and his gangs is only exceeded by his greed for sparkling rubies and diamonds!'

Satisfied, we continued on our way, coming at night to the village of Buckheath, where we encountered something besides the light rain which had begun to fall which put a dent in my companion's good humour.

' "A reward of one hundred pounds" ' I read from the bill posted on the outskirts of the village, ' "to any person or persons who shall discover Claude Delamere and his accomplice, Charley Feather, so as they may be apprehended and convicted." '

Frenchy swore, dismounted, and ripped down the bill from the signpost. 'A hundred pounds!' he spat. 'They mean business, Charley!'

I drew breath and tried to still the trembling of my hands. I had seen the bill shining white in the gathering dusk and approached it warily, guessing that it would most likely concern the recapture of Wild, O'Neill and Mary Brazier. Imagine my initial surprise when I found my own name and Delamere's printed there instead.

'Why do they waste their time on us when Wild is at large?' I gasped at last.

'Aye, and what will happen if your "brother", Robert Major, were to see this?' Frenchy went on, crumpling the paper and casting it aside. 'Will the young scoundrel resist one hundred pounds for the sake of brotherhood, Charley? Tell me that!'

I shook my head and thought grimly of the new possibilities. Which would I choose – to be torn apart by Wild's men, or thrown into the nearest gaol, tried and hanged?

And now the thought of my gold locket secreted about my person, and the value of that locket, and the chance it might offer for me to buy a passage to the New World arose, and I was caught between nightmare and dream.

'Come!' Delamere said roughly. 'We must lie low and make our lodgings under the stars tonight.'

So, deep in gloom, we trudged our horses across rainy fields until we came across a barn which provided shelter for some twenty cows. It was here that we decided to stay until morning.

'No fire tonight,' Delamere groaned, squeezing past the cattle to climb a ladder into a loft alive with rats and spiders. 'No game of cards over a pint of foaming ale.'

I turned my nose up at the foul stench rising from the beasts below. I felt cobwebs cling to my face and the rats scuttle over my feet as I lay my weary body on to the bare boards.

* * *

The stink of cattle filled my nostrils when I woke with the dawn. I heard the tramp of footsteps up the stony lane that led to the barn and quickly roused Delamere who lay beside me.

' 'Tis the cowman!' I hissed, peering through a gap in the boards and spying the bare head of a man dressed in the roughest of fustian coats. 'And his dog!' I added, at the moment when the black and white cur looked up and set up a ferocious barking that would wake the entire county.

The cowman cursed and kicked sideways at the dog, who, however, would not be silent. So, grasping his stout stick, the man must set foot on the ladder himself and come to investigate.

I saw Frenchy go to draw his pistol, but I shook my head and pointed to a narrow exit with a wooden hoist attached, which the cowmen must use to lift hay into the loft. The exit was some twelve feet from the ground – a distance I judged we could jump.

The dog barked and growled, the man's step reached the top of the ladder, and so Frenchy and I leaped.

We landed in a soft, stinking brown slurry, slid and slipped through it and gained terra firma before the man had crossed the loft to gaze down on us. Meanwhile, his cursed dog had run outside and was set on seizing hold of the nearest of us, which happened to be me.

The dog caught me by the ankle and pulled me down. I kicked hard and set myself free, but now the cowman was descending the ladder and running towards me. Frenchy was already in the saddle, tossing my reins towards me, expecting me to catch them and leap on to my horse, which I did with a great effort, this time escaping the dog's jaws. And so we were off.

Across hills, by a river, and then a lake came into view as we headed south. Caked in dirt, besmeared with cow dung, we rode on.

But when we reached the tip of the lake, Frenchy could bear it no longer. 'We will take a dip, Charley!' he cried, leaping from Duke's back and stripping off his jacket and shirt.

I swallowed hard. Here was the tricky problem of stripping off my own clothes, which I must avoid. 'Go!' I urged him. 'Take your swim. I will wait with the horses.'

Frenchy's boots were already off and he was wading into the shallow, reedy water. 'This stench of cattle is more than a man can bear!' he cried, diving headlong and disappearing below the sparkling surface.

I breathed again and looked around me at my companion's cast-off clothes. An oblong shape caught my eye, lying apart from Delamere's shirt, and I soon made out that it was the letter which he kept about him at all times.

What is so important about that letter? I asked myself, idly at first, then beginning to knit my brows in concentration. *Why does Frenchy refuse to part with it, or even to show it to me?*

I thought a while longer, hardly aware of the splashing Delamere made in the water. There the letter lay in the long grass.

I stepped down from my horse and came near to the envelope. I could see a red seal with the imprint of a shield, but had to turn it over to read the address.

I stooped low and picked it up, turned it and read three words, no more, written in a fine lawyer's hand – Thomas Wild, Esquire.

I looked and read again to make sure that the mysterious letter was addressed to none other than Wild himself. And now the question burning in my mind was: *By whom is the letter sent?*

There was no way of answering this unless I broke the seal and opened the envelope, but it could not be done without Frenchy's knowledge.

I hesitated, glanced towards the lake, then let my curiosity overcome me. Recklessly I slipped my fingers under the seal and broke it open. Then I drew the letter from its envelope, opened it out and cast my eyes to the bottom of the page where the bold signature was written.

I gasped then and must read not twice, but three

times the words spread across the page with a great scrawl of black ink, in an elegant, dashing hand: Thomas Pelham-Holles, Duke of Newcastle.

Six

What the letter contains, together with my companion's thoughts thereon. And an occasion for the reader to pass judgement on the politicians of the day.

What business had the worst villain in all England with the Duke of Newcastle, highest in the land? My mind would not comprehend it, and my hand was trembling when Delamere came upon me.

'Villain!' he proclaimed, wading swiftly out of the water and seizing me around the throat.

I could not breathe or swallow, but struggled as manfully as I could. The letter dropped to the ground.

'Thief!' Delamere cried. 'You would pick a man's pocket and betray him, would you!'

I croaked and at last managed to wriggle from his grasp. 'The letter had fallen from your pocket!' I gasped. 'For God's sake, Frenchy, do not kill me!'

'Villain, I don't believe you!' This time he grappled with me, letting out a cry when I landed a kick on his shin. He let go of me then and clutched his leg.

'Believe me or not, I don't care!' I blurted forth, knowing full well that Delamere could not read what he possessed. 'That letter is addressed to Wild, and 'tis written by a great lord of the land!'

At which Frenchy leaves off hopping around and seizes me by the scruff of my neck. 'Thief and liar!' he declares.

My feet are dangling six inches above the ground. He is throttling me.

'Which lord of the land do you mean, you young rogue!'

'Urgh-urhhh!'

'Come, give me the name!'

'Urhhh!'

Frenchy drops me and I draw a rasping breath. 'The Duke of Newcastle.'

'Hah, now I know you lie!'

'I do not, I swear! Thomas Pelham-Holles, Duke of Newcastle, has written this letter to Thomas Wild Esquire.'

And so Frenchy seizes the letter from the ground, which is by now covered in dirt and bespattered with water from the lake.

'The seal was broken,' I lie. 'What harm was done?'

Frenchy raises his fist to make me fall silent. 'This business is none of yours, Charley.'

'Then whose is it? Who besides me will read you the letter without betraying you at last?' I demand, my hands to my throat, rubbing away the pain.

Frenchy shoots me a look. 'You're a devil to sneak around like a thief when my back is turned.'

'And you to keep the letter from me when our lives are at stake and they put up a reward for us both to be hanged!' I protest, full of fiery venom, for I was sick of being called thief and villain by him who was by far the greater thief, and of having my neck squeezed.

At which Frenchy relented and soon decided that since the letter was broken open and did not contain bankers' papers worth thousands of guineas, which was what he had sorely wished – well, there was nothing to do but read and consider its meaning.

'Aye, begin,' Frenchy said, standing well clear of my stinking self.

I commenced the letter. ' "Sir, It has come to the attention of His Majesty's government, and in particular of Sir Robert Walpole, for whom I am Secretary of State for the Southern Department, that a state of lawlessness exists on certain highways, and that there are infamous men who rob travellers in a manner scarce ever known before." '

The writing being close and heavily slanted. I read slowly, until Frenchy lost patience again. 'Damn you, Charley, read on!'

I began again. ' "Neither can we allow a situation in our capital city where fellows who are known to be thieves by the whole kingdom shall, for a long time, rob us, and not only so, but to make jest of us, shall defy the laws and laugh at justice." '

'What will the great Duke do to prevent it?' Frenchy scoffed, listening with interest now.

The writing stretched a long way down the page, so I skipped to what seemed to be the nub. ' "And so I am empowered, as Secretary of State, to offer a pardon to you, Thomas Wild, for all crimes whatsoever committed by you, on whomsoever, whether in town or country, through all the length of this land." '

'What!' Delamere cried. 'The letter promises pardon to the villain. On what condition?'

'Hush,' I told him, tracing my forefinger along the written lines. ' "The pardon to hold good so long as the said Thomas Wild promises to discover each and every one of his agents and apprentices, so the state may try and execute these same felons, and the government may restore law and order to the country by this means." '

I finished reading and looked up at Delamere, who stood in stunned silence. 'That means Heath and Plommer,' I whispered.

'Aye, and O'Neill and Mary, and you and me, Charley. It means every villain who creeps along at night to enter a fine house, every felon who picks a gentleman's pocket. We will all swing from the noose at Tyburn while Wild goes free.'

'But Wild does not have the letter – we do,' I pointed out, holding it as if it were dynamite and would blow up in my hand.

'Which he knows, and most likely he knows the contents too, and so will come after us and descend on us to seize his pardon, which is worth more than all the diamonds in the world put together and stretching from here to China!' Delamere leaned back against a rock overlooking the lake. 'Listen to me, Charley, it now seems certain that Wild's escape on Monday was no accident.'

My head was whirling with the names of the Duke of Newcastle and Sir Robert Walpole, of betrayals and pardons.

'I say the escape was permitted, I would judge even organised, by those higher than the justices in York.'

I spread my hands in a helpless gesture, for who could be higher than the justices of the peace?

Frenchy continued. 'I say that it was the Attorney General who issued the order of habeas corpus to move Wild from York to London, and that he in turn was influenced by the Duke of Newcastle, who wanted Wild free before he could produce this letter of pardon and so implicate the highest politicians in England.'

'The Duke planned the escape? How?'

Frenchy shrugged. 'Perhaps a soldier in the escort party was ordered to provide Wild and O'Neill with pistols. It wouldn't prove difficult. We heard that three soldiers were shot and killed outright.'

'Wild was a danger to the Duke while he remained in gaol?' I thought it through and began to believe it likely, for we had the evidence of the Duke's dishonesty before our eyes.

'And now he's a great danger to us,' Frenchy confirmed, roughly pulling on his shirt and waistcoat, getting ready to ride. ' 'Tis a cruel world, Charley, when the worst man in England has the backing of His Majesty's government!'

And a perilous one – of this I was certain.

So now we pushed our horses to the limit, speaking little as we rode through Cambridgeshire and into Bedfordshire, where the country was populous and so the risks to us rose. So we slept where we might and endured the cold nights of April outdoors.

Once, however, when we came upon a gentleman riding a fine chestnut hunter alone on a country lane, Delamere was sorely tempted. The time was late for a lone traveller, and this one seemed unsteady in the saddle.

'The fool has been drinking at the local inn!' Frenchy exclaimed, concealing himself behind a hayrick. 'My life upon it that he carries a watch and wears a gold ring!'

The gentleman swayed towards us, his horse going at a steady plod under a cloudy sky.

'The foolishness of Man!' Frenchy sighed. 'Here is a halfwit who deserves to be robbed!'

But I laid my hand on his arm. 'He may have companions following hard on his heels. Why risk our necks for a gold ring? And if we steal from him, he will call up the magistrate, there will be a hue and cry, when our lives depend upon us slipping quietly into town.'

Delamere sulked and grumbled, and called me old before my time, but by now the gentleman had passed by, his horse casting a glance in our direction and giving a faint whicker. The rider merely hiccoughed and carried on his befuddled way. Frenchy sighed and set his sights on London once more.

'We will find lodgings north of the river,' he told me, patting the letter tucked into his shirt. 'We will bide our time, listen for news of Wild and his men. Then we will seek out William Plommer.'

I feared for my heart and lungs again at mention of this name. 'What good will that do us?' I cried. 'Plommer is Wild's agent from Clerkenwell to

Blackfriars. There is no alley where he does not hold sway!'

'Until he reads this,' Delamere explained, tapping the letter once more. 'When he sees that Wild means to betray him to save his own neck, his vengeance will be terrible to behold.'

I nodded and considered. ''Tis too dangerous,' I concluded. And I recalled Robert's warning: Trust no one. 'Plommer would as soon shoot us through the heart for our trouble.'

'Believe me, no!' Frenchy protested.

I thought that I caught the first glimpse of city lights spread before us, twinkling under the dark sky. They drew me like a magical charm, and yet repelled me because of the dangers they held.

'This letter makes us powerful!' Frenchy went on. 'With it, we set every villain in London against Wild, our enemy. And then, when Wild is dead at their hands, we go on with our letter to the door of the parliament, and to the Duke of Newcastle himself.'

Inwardly I cried out against this, but said nothing.

'There is a fortune here, Charley! We tell his Lordship that we will take the letter to others in parliament, who will use it against him. We ask him for ten thousand guineas to save his reputation and promise to burn the paper in front of his eyes.'

'Ten thousand guineas!' I echoed faintly.

Delamere rode on, talking of making our fortune, while I, crowded by fears in every direction, made a different plan which did not include my over-ambitious companion.

At dawn we came through Aldgate into the city. I pleaded lameness in my horse and said I could not go on. If Delamere gave me the address of our intended lodgings, I would stable Guinevere close by and follow him on foot.

Edgily, Frenchy agreed to the proposal. 'Come quickly to the Green Man on Paternoster Row by St Paul's,' he told me. 'Ask for Matthew Bayes.'

My heart pounding at my ribs, I made light of my supposed predicament and said I would find Frenchy there.

And that is where I parted ways with Claude Delamere, the most gallant of highwaymen, and sought a way out of the circumstance in which he had landed me.

First, I tethered Guinevere within an empty coach-house, then went in search of a good laundress, up early to hang out her washing.

I found one by and by, neatly pegging out petticoats, bustling about her yard. Waiting until she went back into the house, I climbed the wall and chose a petticoat, skirt and bodice closest to my own size, whipped them from the line and made my exit before the good woman returned with a second laden basket.

I heard her set up a cry when she discovered the gaps I had made in her neat row, but by then I was down the alleyway and across the street back to the coach-house, where I went about my transformation.

Off came the breeches and waistcoat, on went the petticoats and light brown skirt under Guinevere's steady gaze. I kept on my boy's shirt, but loosened it at the neck and covered it with a dark-blue bodice which I laced down the front with clumsy fingers. As for my hair, shorn of its curls a week ago and which only now began to grow back, I could do nothing.

Strange to feel the girl's bodice pinch my waist and the long skirt flounce about my legs. The new clothes felt damp and uncomfortable, though they smelled clean and no doubt utterly changed my appearance. For this is what I wanted as I bade my mare a sad farewell and set sail from the coach-house – a new Charley Feather whom no man would recognise. A fresh start, away from Delamere.

While they hunted high and low for a Frenchman and a youth with a feather in his hat, I would be passing through London as Charlotte Sharpe, a demure maid, skirt swishing along the pavement, looking for a lonely widow – a kind mistress who would take me in and train me in cross-stitch, and make me her sweet companion in a life of perfect refinement, far from the world of Thomas Wild and the highwaymen I had known.

Seven

*In which my hopes of a kind widow are soon
dashed and I am reintroduced to the manners of
London society, including my first position as
maid in the house of Mr G.*

I made my way from Aldgate up into Spitalfields, eager
to hold my skirt high and keep it out of the mire – for
I must present myself as a respectable maid worthy of
good employment – until a passing boy laughed at my
leather riding boots and I had to drop my hem to
conceal the manly attire.

Ahead lay the great markets of Spitalfields. Behind
was a set of cast-off clothes and a three-cornered hat
bearing a plume of white feathers.

Besides, I had much to do, pushing my way through
jostling crowds of fishmongers and bakers, fruit-sellers
and servants sent forth early from the grand houses to
buy fresh meat.

'What do you lack, mistress?' came the cry from
many a doorway. 'Here we have pies crammed full of

the finest game birds, salted hams and freshly killed hares!'

Or, 'Buy a penny loaf from a poor boy, Miss!'

And, 'Spices from the Orient – mace, nutmeg and cinnamon to flavour your plain English dishes!'

Ignoring them all, I pushed bravely on, keeping to the centre of the streets and holding my head high so as not be distracted by the orphan beggars huddled under overhanging roofs, crying for scraps and being kicked for their pains, for I knew I was but a hair's breadth from adding to their number.

During my highway travels I had forgotten the noises of the streets – the heavy trundle of cartwheels, the clip of horses' hooves and the raised voices of people going about their business. But I had lived long enough in the seething city to know not to pause or dawdle, lest a pickpocket took his chance or a bully found occasion to pick a fight. And so I hurried on.

On Bishop's Court, off Gun Street, I entered a draper's shop and closed the door on the hustle and bustle outside. The elderly woman who kept the shop was a homely, sedate figure, busily winding a strip of lace around a card, surrounded by ribbons, gloves and fabrics of every hue. She regarded me without interest, then asked me abruptly what I would buy.

'That is not why I am here,' I begin, which

straightaway puts a frown on the old lady's face. 'I am seeking a position in a grand house.'

'And so are a hundred girls,' she retorts. 'And many are more likely-looking than you.'

I bite my tongue, reckoning that I must indeed seem odd, with my shorn head and bulky boy's shirt tucked down inside my blue bodice. 'Have you heard of a lady seeking a maid?' I persist. 'I am willing to work hard.'

'Are you honest?' she demands, making as if to stab me with the pointed end of her bobbin.

'As the day,' I say swiftly, gazing at her without flinching.

'Where is your home?' asks Mistress Draper.

I hesitate a second over this, not having prepared an answer.

'Ha!' she cries. 'The girl has no home, yet says she is honest. Ha again!'

'Do you know of a lady?' I demand, disliking the new tone. 'If you do not, please be so good as to tell me and let me be on my way.'

At this, the draper woman shrieks with laughter. 'I think you should not put on airs, with your "honest as the day" and your "please be so good", for I see you are no better than a street girl!'

Seeing that I will get no help here, I return the lady's fire. 'Nor you,' I tell her, 'with your cheap lace and bedraggled ribbons, and your old, ugly face!'

'Ah!' she cries, turning and calling out a man's name as I leave, slamming the door behind me.

And I did not regret pronouncing her ugly, for she had called me 'street girl' when I was trying to better myself and become a lady's maid.

The morning progressed in a hum and bustle, but the next event of any account on my first day in Spitalfields came about in this manner.

I was looking into a baker's window, lured by the smell from the ovens, for I had had no breakfast, when I felt a small girl take me by the hand and cry out that she had lost her mother. The child was no more than six years old, her face grimy and smeared with tears.

For a moment my heart softened, but then I recalled the old trick, and sure enough when I looked around I saw an accomplice, no more than eight years of age, creeping up behind and attempting to softly slide his fingers between the folds of my skirt where he thought a purse might be hidden.

I snatched my hand out of the girl's grasp and turned on the boy, giving him a kick and thrusting him from me. 'Thief!' I cried out, glad that I had hidden my gold locket down the front of my bodice when I had furtively changed my clothes in the stall of the empty coach-house.

'Thief! Thief!' The cry went up.

But the felons being small and nimble, they darted away and were soon lost between the clattering wheels of carts and coaches.

'I see you give as good as you get,' said a burly bystander, admiring my rough way with the lad. ' 'Twas a hefty kick you landed, my maid!'

I straightened my bodice and adopted a modest air. 'Sir, do you know of any fine lady who seeks a servant?' I asked the gentleman, as I had done all morning, of anyone who would stop to listen.

My eyes were cast down, then slowly I allowed them to rise up the length of his figure until I met his scarred face and found that I was talking to none other than Joseph Fielder, a cutpurse and well-known member of William Plommer's gang, who, as bad luck would have it, knew me of old.

'A fine lady seeking a servant?' the villain echoed, eyeing me carefully, searching in his memory for where he might have seen me before, though the skirt and bodice seemed to confuse him.

I could not very well flee, for this would arouse suspicion, so I nodded and held his gaze.

Luckily for me, a man on a bay horse came riding by, breaking news that sent shudders through the crowded street.

'Thomas Wild is in town!' he cried. 'He is back, with O'Neill at his side!'

I gasped and leaned against the shop window for support, then watched as Joseph Fielder seized the reins of the bay horse and accosted its rider. 'Is there a reward out for Wild's capture?' he demanded.

'None!' the rider replied. 'Wild has evaded justice and returned to his old haunts by the river. They say he will drink the blood of the Frenchman, Delamere, and any who aid him!'

'Ha, there is a feud broken out between them!' Fielder laughed delightedly. 'What will Wild pay for Delamere's head, I wonder!'

I knew I must not stay to hear more, so, regaining my wits, I looked around me and chose an alley down which to make my escape. Behind me, every man and woman on the street talked of Wild's return.

'Twas a good plan of mine, to desert Frenchy and put on a maid's clothing. Thus I reflected as I sought shelter that evening in Bishopsgate churchyard by St Botolph's church. Never had I such need of secrecy and disguise as I did in this dangerous time.

Still, I was cold and hungry as I crept between the monuments to the dead. Bats flew about me, flickering shapes between the stone crosses. I lay down to sleep on a flat tomb covered in moss, in a quiet corner sheltered by an overhanging yew tree.

What of Mary? I wondered. I had heard no mention

of her since the notorious escape six days before, except that she had fled along with Wild and O'Neill. In my half-waking state, I recalled her teasing eyes, and how she called me a cold fish, and how her red dress came low on her bosom where she stored small items, and I remembered how she carried me in half dead from the street and fed me, and then my eyes filled with tears to think that I might never see her again.

I curled on my stone bed, drawing my knees to my chest for extra warmth.

And that was how the verger of St Botolph's found me early next morning, for it was a Sunday and he had come to tend the church.

'Child,' he said gently, putting his hand on my shoulder. 'Have you no home, nor mother nor father to go to?'

I jumped up then. 'I am no child!' I protested, seeing that I was a match for the frail old man. Long, grey hair trailed over his high collar, though the top of his head was bald. His face was thin, his nose large, his watery eyes half hidden by spectacles.

He nodded and beckoned me to follow across the churchyard to the small lodge by the church gate.

I hesitated, but only for a moment. The verger seemed intent on showing me kindness – perhaps his act of charity on this, the Sabbath.

Sure enough, inside the low cottage he sat me down by his fire and gave me warm milk and bread to dip in it. He asked me how I came to be without a roof, and when I shook my head and allowed tears to come into my eyes, he did not press me. I felt free to confess then that I was an honest girl seeking employment and would be pleased if he could point to a member of the morning's congregation who might require a maid.

This good man's name was John, and he instructed me to wait in his cottage until after the minister had given the morning service, when he would make inquiries on my behalf and then come to fetch me.

I did as he bade me, taking stock of the poor, plain furniture, the earth floor and the low beams of the ceiling. Through the narrow window I heard the lusty singing of the morning worshippers, and then the minister's interminable sermon, delivered in a voice that made me drowsy and almost sent me to sleep again by the verger's fire.

Then I heard the door-latch lift and John came in with a small, round gentleman with dark, curled hair, almost as wide as he was tall, richly dressed in an embroidered waistcoat and fine frock-coat, wearing a ruby ring on one plump finger.

'This is Mr G,' John began. I will not give the gentleman's name, because of what is to occur. 'He has a house on Broad Street, not far from here. It seems his maidservant has left him without warning and he might offer you a place if he finds that you suit him.'

I jumped up eagerly, thanking kind John, and saying to myself that Mr G must be an honest man who came to church and visited a good tailor for his clothes.

Mr G looked me up and down. 'She is small,' he murmured to John.

'But strong!' I assured him. 'I can work from dawn to dusk. I am never sick.'

'You have no family, child?' Mr G asked me.

I shook my head. 'I must make my own way in the world.'

He came then and turned me around, looked at me this way and that. 'There is a Mrs G,' he told me, 'but she is sickly and keeps to her chamber. You must answer to me instead.'

At this I nodded. I smiled at John and thanked him sincerely, said that God would bless him for this kind act.

Mr G remarked that, upon reflection, I would do, and promptly took me from the churchyard on to Broad Street where the houses were tall and clean and white. And so I found my first employment with Mr G, a sugar merchant.

Eight

*Containing a distressing scene which the faint-hearted
reader may pass over, and a lesson learned.*

I marched after Mr G up some broad steps and through
a wide door decorated with curved glass panels, into an
oak-panelled hallway where we were greeted by the stout
figure of Eleanor Jenkins, housekeeper.

Mr G handed me over without a word, and that was
the only time I expected to see the fine front of the
house, for Mrs Jenkins conveyed me up the back stairs
to the attics and said I must sleep under the eaves and
be up before dawn to do my master's bidding.

'And what will be my duties?' I inquired as cheerfully
as I could, determined to make the most of the change
in my fortunes.

'Your duties are to do as you are bid,' Mrs Jenkins
replied, closing the door of the small room and, to my
surprise, turning the key in the lock after her.

This left me time to look around me at the straw
mattress on the floor and the small window set into the

sloping ceiling. There was no grate for a fire, nor chair nor table to sit at.

After an hour or so, Mrs Jenkins returned with clean linen and new shoes for me and a basin of cold water to bathe myself in. She waited by the door for me to begin.

But I stood my ground. 'I will not undress while you watch,' I said firmly.

She smiled without mirth. 'As you wish,' she said, withdrawing to the corridor, where I heard her pace up and down.

Thinking that she might yet disturb me, I heaved at the mattress and dragged it up against the doorway, and with my modesty thus secure, I began to unlace.

'Do you have a name, girl?' the housekeeper called from outside the room.

'Charlotte,' I replied, which sounded strange on my tongue. I stood in my clean shift, shivering as I splashed the water over my arms and face.

'Well, Charlotte, you must make haste. The master wishes to instruct you in the ways of the household and must not be kept waiting.'

So I dressed quickly, discarding my boy's shirt and donning a short, fitted cream jacket over my shift and bodice. Then I put on dainty laced shoes, straightened out the gathers of my full skirt, ruffled up my petticoats and sallied forth.

Down we went to Mr G's library, past a room on the first floor that Mrs Jenkins pointed out as the mistress's bedchamber. 'You may not enter there,' she said sternly, tapping the keys hanging from her waist. 'The door is kept locked on Mr G's orders.'

This house seemed full of keys and locked doors, I reflected. 'What ails her?' I ventured to ask as the housekeeper swept along the corridor.

But Mrs Jenkins only put a warning finger to her lips. 'God in His mercy give her grace,' she whispered.

Mad, I concluded. *Out of her wits and locked away from the world. A wild and frenzied madness which the doctors cannot tame.* I pictured a black-haired lunatic with a sullen brow, a laughing, snarling madwoman, and the idea sent a shiver down my spine.

And then we were at the library door, where the housekeeper melted away and left me alone to knock and learn my duties.

I entered at my master's command.

Mr G came and closed the door behind me, then went to sit at his desk, though no book lay open before him. He glanced up and appraised my appearance, noting the close-fitting jacket and the frill of white linen at my neck. 'Much improved,' he observed. 'Come here, girl.'

I approached and stood on the opposite side of the great desk.

'Can you curtsey, girl?' Mr G inquired, studying me closely throughout.

I dropped an uncertain curtsey and rose with a wobble.

'No, the maid cannot curtsey,' he concluded. 'Can you fetch and carry?'

'Yes, sir.'

'Can you run to the butcher for meat and to the baker for bread?'

'Yes, sir.' The sight of so many leather-bound volumes on shelves reaching to the ceiling widened my eyes with wonder at the knowledge they contained. I let my glance stray from Mr G.

'Can you make your master content?' he asked, catching me by surprise by striding to my side of the desk.

At first I did not understand his meaning, for any such idea was far from my thoughts. But when the master grabbed my waist with his fat hand and pulled me against his belly, why then I would have cried out, but that he put his other hand firmly across my mouth.

'Come girl, you are not so prim!' he exclaimed crossly, for I had attempted to bite that hand. 'Understand that your duties in this house go beyond sweeping the floors. You are here to please me in any way I choose.'

At which I snatched myself away from his grasp and from his hot breath upon my neck. 'Do not touch me, sir!' I cried out, running to the furthest part of the room, thinking that this was no true Christian behaviour and that John had but poor judgement of his congregation.

But my master pursued me with a savage look, saying that I must obey or be whipped. This was not a fair bargain and I must think quickly. I must measure a risk and take it for the sake of my honour. 'You will be sorry if you proceed,' I warned, backing towards the window.

Mr G laughed, lunged at me once more and said he would call for Mrs Jenkins to give me medicine that would tame me.

And I then I realised that the tight-lipped housekeeper had known what my duties were from the start, and I cursed her for putting me in the master's way.

'Still you will be sorry!' I insisted. Which gave my attacker pause for thought, though he still held me fast.

I noted the casement window which stood ajar. 'Is there not something strange in my appearance?' I went on, struggling to unclasp Mr G's hands from around my waist.

'How, strange?' His small eyes narrowed and almost disappeared behind the folds of his fleshy cheeks.

'My hair,' I went on, thrusting my red-gold crop in his face.

'Short,' he grunted. 'Aye, that is odd in a maid.'

'And my boots when you found me in the verger's cottage?'

'Riding boots,' he reflected slowly, his lip beginning to curl in disgust. 'God's truth, do I understand what you are saying?'

I nodded then, holding my breath, praying for time. 'Aye, I am no maid,' I told him boldly. 'But Charley Feather, lately come to London from the highway with the Frenchman, Claude Delamere, intent on stealing from the rich for the sake of their Christian soul, for remember, " 'Tis harder for a rich man to enter Heaven that it is for a camel to pass through the eye of a needle!" '

'By God, no!' Mr G cried, letting me go and recoiling in horror. ' 'Tis a youth dressed in woman's clothing. He has come to rob us all!'

I laughed out loud as he ran on his fat legs to the door and fumbled with the lock. His face was red and sweating, his chest heaving and his breath coming hard as I climbed on to the window sill and judged the drop into the street below. 'May God punish you with plague and pestilence!' I vowed before I leaped.

'Spare me!' Mr G bellowed as the key dropped on to the carpet and he fell to his knees. 'Do not kill me. Take my watch. Take my ring, my candlesticks and plate. Only spare my life!'

From which you may judge that my sugar merchant

was a lecherous coward, and you must pray to God that he is revealed in his true colours before harm may come to any other maid.

And so I learned my lesson not to enter blind the employment of a fine gentleman, but to seek a safer berth in the future, whatever that might hold.

Nine

In which I am forced into the underbelly of our great city and experience a low point in my fortunes. I find a new employer and encounter two old friends.

'Wild's bullies are everywhere!' A great whisper ran through the streets. 'They beat men to death and drop their bloodied bodies into the Thames.'

'What is the matter?' Women gossiping in shop doorways picked up scraps of news and passed it on.

'They say Wild has been betrayed by one of his own. Nothing will stop him from wreaking his revenge!'

I shuddered when I heard such things and passed on hurriedly. Sometimes I saw the evidence with my own eyes – a knot of men lurking down an alley, slouched against the filthy walls, awaiting their next victim. And so I would swish my skirts and sail by, trembling inwardly but placing my faith in my new guise.

'And how did Wild escape the noose in York?' they asked in taverns and on market stalls.

'He got gunpowder and broke through the walls of the county gaol,' some lads bragged. They talked of explosion and fire, of twenty killed by the smoke and of Wild shooting ten more men dead.

Or, 'He paid his gaoler twenty guineas, donned a disguise and walked free without exchanging a single blow.'

Or else, 'Wild's men gathered in great numbers and stormed the gaol. One hundred soldiers could do nothing to prevent the escape.'

The greater the lie, the more people believed it to be true. But the only part of the gossip that I took to heart were the words that dropped from every man's lips, which were, 'Of one thing you may be certain; no man may sleep safe until the feud is settled.'

Thus I flitted through a whole week without a home or a soul to talk to. I lived how I could, sinking deeper into that state I thought I had left behind for ever, though I refused to beg, as my pride would not let me, and only stole what I needed to keep body and soul together – for to steal for profit was to risk arrest, which I feared now more than death itself. And always I kept that locket about me.

And here I confess freely that I had not felt so low since I left Bess in Southampton and returned to London, which was, as you know, three whole years before. 'Tis a wearying sensation to be alone and in danger, to be seeking shelter and finding none to offer it, trusting no one.

Sometimes the ache I felt around my heart threatened to rise as tears when I pictured Bess in her new life: married, if Robert was to be believed, and a world away from these mean streets. Bess had blue skies above her now, and miles of fields and mountains at her feet. I wished her luck and longed to be with her.

Instead, I crept through the maze of streets, sliding south, day by day, to the river and the great tower, then veering north again when I caught sight of Tyburn Hill across the water, and saw three felons hanging in chains until the crows had pecked out their eyes and their corpses had rotted. And so I kept to the area by St Paul's, and fell in at last with Sara Wheeler, an ancient woman of some seventy years, who owned a pawnbroker's shop on Ludgate Hill.

Age and infirmity made it necessary for Sara to have a servant about her as her eyes and ears, and this was the only reason she took me in and fed me my first wholesome meal for more than seven days.

Sara herself is as wizened as a walnut, with a dry complexion and wisps of white hair falling over her face. She wears tiny spectacles and a man's greatcoat, even in summer. A rare glimpse of foot and ankle reveals legs swollen with dropsy, which goes ill with her skinny frame.

'I may be almost deaf,' she warned, lest I cross her, 'and my eyes are dimmer than a moldiwarp's, but I have a sharp brain and tongue to match.'

'What became of your last girl?' I asked, mindful of my recent experience with Mr G.

I had come across my new employer as she struggled to carry a jug of ale from a tavern and I came from the Inns of Court, where I had hoped and failed to find service. I had offered assistance, thinking that I might help myself to a drop or two of the jug's contents when the old woman's back was turned. One thing had led to another, and within five minutes I had secured myself a position.

'My last girl was Moll, and she threw herself into the arms of a drayman and married him.' Sara slammed down a platter of bread and salt beef before me. 'I warned her that marriage meant a life of servitude repaid by ingratitude, if you were lucky and by blows and curses if you were not.'

'But she didn't listen?' I asked, gratefully cramming meat into my mouth.

'Speak up!' Sara demanded.

'She married him anyway?'

'Louder!'

I swallowed then shouted as loud as I could. 'I have no plans to marry!'

At which Sara Wheeler opened her mouth wide and cackled and laughed until I thought she would choke.

And so I settled into my new life of cleaning, polishing, scrubbing and sweeping, for my mistress waged a battle against dust to protect her precious silver and pewter, her clocks and watches, silk purses decorated with pearls and all the gold chains and gems which lined her shelves.

I laboured hard. Sara fed and clothed me. April turned to May without event.

'Charlotte, lay the fire!' my mistress would cry from her upstairs room at five o'clock each morning.

I would rise from my mattress under the counter, stretch my stiff limbs and go to fetch kindling from the yard. Working the bellows to fan the flames would warm me a little; then, by the time my mistress emerged, the kettle would be boiling on the fire, and I would be out of the house to fetch meat. By seven, I was polishing silver plates until they shone like mirrors. By noon, I would have driven the spiders from the corners and banished them to the cellars. In the afternoon, the polishing began anew.

And so I discovered, like many another poor girl, that the life of a maidservant is no better than slavery, and I did miss the open road and the birds singing in the trees.

But I watched and learned. I saw sly men in dirty, worn coats bring lace handkerchiefs and embroidered purses to my mistress. Furtive maids would carry in small items of fine china stolen from their mistress's cupboards. Sara would weigh and value the objects, offer less than half of their worth, then argue brazenly until the customer gave way. Once secured, the item would remain for ever with my mistress – for it is hunger that drives a person to Madam Poverty, and once in her grip, she seldom releases her hold.

'You may be sure that no one leaves here satisfied!' Sara would cackle, as if sharing a huge jest.

There is no love lost between Sara Wheeler and myself, though she did not mistreat me, but was severe in any case.

One evening in mid-June, when Sara demanded ale, I took to the street with an empty jug. I felt easier in my skirt and petticoats now that my hair had begun to grow back in soft curls which fell about my face. As I walked in the warm air, I was thinking of Delamere on the morning we had parted. 'Come to the Green Man on Paternoster Row,' he had said. 'Ask for Matthew Bayes.'

Curiosity drew me there now, since, though the city

had been turned upside down by Wild's men, Frenchy had managed to lay low. *Perhaps he has changed his plan and slipped away from the city*, I thought to myself, determined, against my better judgement, to find out more.

And so I went into the Green Man on Paternoster Row, which was not far from where I lived, and ordered ale, thinking that if I stood at the counter I would soon glean news.

Sure enough, a group of men and women, together with a fair girl of about eight years, were gathered around a table in a dark corner. They chatted merrily enough until the conversation turned to more serious matters.

'How is it possible that the Frenchman can stay hidden?' one man asks. 'Wild tears the city apart to find him.'

I feel the hairs at the back of my neck rise at this, and I steady myself against the counter.

'Aye, and it cannot be mere jewels and banker's notes that drive him,' another adds. 'What are a few diamond pins to a man like Wild?'

'It is more than money,' a woman confirms, and, to my amazement, I recognise the voice of Mary Brazier.

I half turn and see Mary in profile, almost running to her then to embrace her, but I hold myself still.

'They say it is a secret paper that Frenchy stole,' a third man says, rising from the table to take his leave.

'Worth more than a king's ransom, though only Delamere knows what it contains,' Mary tells him. Then she turns to the girl and says, 'Hannah, my dear, you must go with Jeremy and take this parcel of linen to Mistress Osborne by Blackfriars Bridge.'

The girl I had noted earlier stood up beside the man. 'What am I to tell her?' she asks in a bright, innocent voice, taking the brown package and tucking it under her arm.

'That she must take out the work which shows the letters B and N, so that the linen cannot be traced,' Mary instructs.

And I know now that Mary has taken in another orphan child, just as I had been taken in three years before, that she has made her useful, and that Hannah will be looked after and taught the ways of the world by Mary, just as I was.

At which I would have cried, but that the innkeeper finished pouring the frothing ale into my jug and handed it to me, asking for payment. I gave him the money and slipped out on to the street after the girl and the man.

I stared hard at the girl without fear of recognition. She was small and undersized as I had been, but her hair was the colour of straw. She had large grey eyes and a full, pretty mouth, and she took the hand of the man, Jeremy, as they turned towards the river.

And then I almost ran back into the inn, to speak with my old friend Mary, except that I glanced in the window and saw a face that struck terror in me, almost as much as if it had been Wild himself.

The face was broad and marked by the pox, reddish-blue in colour, with watery eyes. He spoke, and though I could not hear him, I knew that the voice would emerge as a hoarse whisper and that there would be a livid mark on his neck where they had cut the noose from him.

O'Neill! He slammed his mug on the table, stabbing his finger at Mary, who drew back from him. He rose, took her by the arm and remonstrated with her, shaking her hair loose with the violence of his action. She pleaded with him but he threw her down roughly on to the bench, where a second woman tried to calm her. Meanwhile, Patrick O'Neill was making for the door.

'Damn the woman!' he snarled as he burst into the street. 'Her loose tongue will be the death of us!'

I cowered back against the wall, glad of his anger, for he did not look about him as he went, and so he had no chance to recognise me.

But I trembled nevertheless, and I went home with a sore heart. I had observed Mary and found myself ousted from her affections. I had seen O'Neill, and hated and feared him more than ever.

* * *

I grew afraid of every shadow around every corner. Fear kept me from my food and drink, so that my mistress declared I ate less than a mouse and grew pale.

'What ails you, girl?' she would ask, prodding me in my ribs and peering at me with her short-sighted eyes.

I confessed that I missed the country from whence I came, and in this way began to prepare her for our parting.

I had begun to make a firm plan to leave London again and make my way westwards towards Oxford, which was a city I had heard something of, but where I trusted no one would know of the fine highwayman, Claude Delamere, and his young companion, Charley Feather.

To make the journey I must have money to travel by coach, and it was now that I must earn all I could from the sale of my little gold locket. So I went about and found a pawnbroker named Christopher Swift, determined to drive a hard bargain.

Swift's shop lay by the river in an out-of-the-way place which backed on to the wharves and so smelled of foul water and rotting fish. The courtyard where it stood was close and dark, the shop doorway scarcely noticeable between high stacks of fishermen's baskets.

I approached cautiously, holding my breath against the stench. Once inside, I made out that Swift cared nothing for dust or cobwebs, and that even the rats had free reign to scuttle along shelves of dull and tarnished wares. Swift himself, a young man of not more than twenty, wearing a filthy waiscoat and stained yellow breeches, sat in a corner smoking a pipe.

'I wish to know the value of this locket,' I declared, holding it in the palm of my hand.

Swift sprang forward with surprising speed, snatched it from me and studied it beneath a magnifying glass. 'Tut-tut-tut,' he said with a shake of his head, then turning it over, said, 'Tut' again.

' 'Tis of fine quality!' I began to protest, seeing that the pawnbroker was intent on playing me as a fool.

But then the door burst open and a second customer entered.

'How do you do, Kit!' the new arrival declared. 'I have plate for you here in this sack, and in my pocket a sapphire ring.'

Swift nodded easily. He began to tell me that my locket was of inferior quality and that the inscribed initials made it difficult to sell on, but I had closed my ears and demanded the return of the item.

'Hold!' Swift protested, turning the locket and beginning to soften. ' 'Tis a pretty thing, after all.'

'Give it to me!' I urged breathlessly.

'Yes, give it!' The newcomer laughed. ' 'Tis in the nature of Woman to change her mind!'

If I had been unsure at first about the identity of my supporter, I now knew it in my heart's core. *Do not turn and reveal yourself!* I thought. *Do not speak. Do not let yourself be recognised!*

Having secured the locket, I would have slid out of the shop, except that the door was held open for me; a face was smiling at me, a young man was bowing before me. I hastened past.

'By God, I cannot believe my eyes!' the voice said.

I hurried on into the courtyard.

Footsteps followed me. 'Turn!' the youth begged. 'Stay to talk. I am Robert Major, and you are . . .'

Aye, 'twas him indeed. And I had picked up my skirt and begun to run, down an alleyway, out on to the wharf side. I saw the dull brown water of the River Thames run sluggishly by.

But Robert followed me. 'You are . . . No, you cannot be!'

I stumbled against a heavy anchor chain coiled on the cobbles and almost fell.

Robert helped me to stand. 'You are Charley Feather!' he declared, looking straight into my eyes. 'By God, Charley, what are you wearing?'

'Do not tell!' I begged. 'Upon your life, do not say you have seen me!'

' 'Tis you!' He laughed, looking me up and down, and he could tell by the way I wore my clothes and by my shape that I was indeed a girl. 'Why, Charley, you have fooled us all!'

I nodded and held my head up high. 'What say you now?' I demanded.

'I say, by God!' Robert grinned, walking a full circle around me. 'But did I not say you were too slender and lacked muscle?'

'Aye, but you did not guess my secret,' I returned, feeling my colour rise and cursing my pale complexion for letting it show. 'I picked a pocket and rode the highway with the best of them, did I not?'

'Charley, I am amazed!' he admitted. 'And now I come to look, you are a comely sight and may make a good wench in time.'

At which I sprang forward to box Robert's ears, for I would not have the fairer sex spoken of so lightly.

He fended me off and laughed again. 'Be more ladylike,' he teased, 'else you will never secure a husband!'

'All the better!' I retorted. 'For I will never place my trust in the hands of a man who prattles of love but acts as a gaoler to his wife and shackles her to a brood of little ones while he drinks at the alehouse!'

'Well spoken, Charley!' Robert applauded. 'I see womanhood has not dulled your spirit.'

I calmed myself then, and asked him if in truth he had ever suspected me of the lie, especially when we lived a family life with Bess.

'Not once, Charley,' he assured me with a wink, then sidled up close. 'But I mean to make up for it now.'

I pushed him away. 'What do you mean?'

'To treat you like a girl, to squeeze your waist and steal a kiss, no less!'

At which I raised the flat of my hand as if to smack his face, but Robert caught hold of my wrist and did as he had promised, leaning forward and landing a sound kiss on my cheek.

I fell silent, and so did he.

Then he blushed and begged my pardon, looked contrite and stepped back and stumbled against the chain, as I had done.

I helped him up. 'In all seriousness . . .' I began.

'Yes, Charley?'

'In all seriousness, you will keep my secret?'

Robert nodded. 'You know that you are in danger still?' he whispered, looking about as if the wharf had ears.

'I know that Wild's men are everywhere.'

'But more than that. Delamere's blood is up. He wants you dead, Charley.'

'Ah!' I had not foreseen this – that Frenchy, too, would see me as a traitor and turn so much against me. 'How do you know?'

'He sends word into the streets, promising fifty

guineas to anyone who can bring you to him. What have you stolen from him, that he pursues you so?'

'I stole nothing!' I declared. 'But I know a great secret, Robert.'

'Which is?'

I was drawn to tell him, and for a moment the words lay on the tip of my tongue. But then I recalled Robert's own piece of advice to me some months before. 'Trust no one!' I reminded him.

'Ha, but 'tis me, Charley!' he protested. 'We are on the same side, you and I!'

I shook my head. ' 'Tis too dangerous to share the knowledge.'

'To me or to you?' he asked, talking low, looking straight into my eyes.

'To both. I would not burden you with what I learned from a certain letter, Robert, and neither would I put myself in your hands.'

'You are hard-hearted to deny me,' he accused. Then, with more spirit and with the old, laughing curl of his lips he continued, 'I would defend you with my life, Shar-lee!'

'Do not tease me,' I protested, determined to walk away now, and more than ever set upon my plan of gaining money and leaving London. 'Robert, for the sake of our old friendship, tell no one of this meeting.'

He sighed, then nodded. He moved towards me as if

to take my hand and perhaps to kiss me on the lips. I hesitated, but caught my breath and turned away. Then I ran quickly along the wharf and slipped down a dark passage, leaving Robert deep in thought.

Ten

We leave behind all romantic notions on the bank of the River Thames. I learn another harsh lesson on human nature, namely that we must look out for ourselves, for no other man will, and that a delicate conscience is a dangerous thing.

Robert Major did not attempt to follow me to my lodging, where my mistress greeted me with suspicion.

'Where have you been? You are breathing hard, you smell of the wharves and river,' she accused me. 'Methinks you had a tryst – you have been playing the flirt!'

I denied it strongly.

'Pah, you are like Moll and all the rest,' she sneered. ' 'Tis an old story. A young girl will sniff out courtship like a hound smells the fox. You will fall into a young man's arms and so I will be deserted.'

'I will do nothing of the sort!' I proclaimed, my heart still secretly sore from the imploring looks Robert had given me. I was half sorry now that I had not placed my trust in him and let him kiss me, though Reason told me I had acted wisely.

And I thought how strange it must seem for him to see me in my maid's guise, and to turn from wrestling and back-slapping with Charley Feather to blushes and soft looks with Charlotte.

Sara saw my preoccupation and instantly bade me busy myself by taking a pail into the cellar and going down upon my hands and knees to scrub the stone floor. Then, for several days, she kept me working at the worst tasks without pause from morn until night, so that my hands were blistered, and this was as if she meant to punish me for my youth, strength and comely looks. For she was an ancient woman who had never found a husband, and would take her bitterness with her to the grave.

There came a Friday morning late in May when my sour mistress banished me to the upstairs chamber, where I brooded about my lack of success in gaining money for my passage to Oxford.

I looked down upon the street, thinking that I must gather my courage at last to close the narrow shop door for the last time and go forth into the world – Delamere and Wild notwithstanding – when I saw two tall figures pause beneath the window.

'This is the place,' one said, pointing to my mistress's doorway.

The other cast a quick and furtive look up and down the street, which was full at that time of tradesmen pushing carts, youths lurking on corners, and plainly-dressed women hurrying about their masters' business.

I saw the baker's boy spy the two strangers and step back into the shadow of the house opposite. I saw a woman turn to her neighbour and whisper a short phrase. And though the men wore hats and I could only view them from above, I knew from the startled reaction in the street that they were Wild's men.

My heart thumped, thinking that by some means they had discovered me and meant to take me. I was cornered like a rat, expecting any moment to hear heavy footsteps on the stair.

The silence in the small room where my mistress slept seemed to thicken. I thought to hide myself under the bed, even to fling myself from the window and risk landing in the street below.

But then the murmur of voices conveyed to me a different message, and I lay down with my ear to the floorboards to hear better.

'The old woman cannot hear,' one man was saying to his companion with a mocking laugh. Then he shouted loud into her ear. 'Come, mistress, what news?'

'News worth a hundred guineas, and I would see your money before we proceed,' Sara told him boldly.

At which there was a scuffle, and I could see through

my slit between the boards that my mistress had been thrust back against her counter, and that Wild's men were no respecters of age or infirmity.

'We proceed, as you say, but at our own pace and on our own terms,' the first and heavier of the men sneered. He had removed his hat and I could see the bald top of his head and the silver gleam of a pistol against Sara's chest.

'Your news!' the second prompted, standing back to finger the polished plates on Sara's shelves. 'You say it is of Delamere?'

I gasped and put my hand to my mouth.

'Aye, the Frenchman,' my mistress hissed, finding herself trapped with a gun to her heart by her greed for the reward Wild had offered.

'How do you have news of him?' the second man asked.

'Thieves and villains come to me here to sell what they have stolen; they talk carelessly about their business. I listen. Often they forget I am here.'

'And so?' the more calm and patient of the two men asked.

'And so I have heard tell that Delamere lodges not far from here, in a manner that keeps his identity safe.'

'Good!' The man with the gun seemed better pleased. 'Now you must tell us the name of the house.'

' 'Tis written on a piece of paper kept locked in a place nearby,' Sara replied, not flinching under his brutal gaze.

Hearing this, I understood that my mistress might add the quality of cunning to her greed.

'Play no games. Tell us the Frenchman's lodging!' the brutish villain urged angrily, raising the pistol to her temple.

'I will not. You must pay me one hundred guineas, or else blow out my brains.'

And seeing that Sara Wheeler did not care to be bullied, the slighter man proceeded to bargain with her, offering her twenty guineas now – which was a great deal of money and all he carried with him – if she would but lead them to the piece of paper containing Delamere's address.

'One hundred,' Sara insisted. 'If Wild wants the Frenchman's head on a plate, he must pay me in full first.'

There was much swearing then, and a scuffle between the two men, which ended with the bald one knocking Sara to the ground and his companion setting her back on her feet and telling her she must wait until evening, when they would return with her money.

'The old harridan holds the advantage over us,' the calculating man said as they walked out into the street.

'Aye, until we lay hold of Delamere's address,' the

other agreed. 'After which, we may drown her for a witch in the Thames!' And he laughed loudly and strode ahead.

And now my conscience pricked me sorely and I could not keep myself still, but would fidget up and down the stairs, trying to keep out of my mistress's path, for she was in a sour temper throughout the afternoon, with 'Charlotte this' and 'Charlotte that', and all to keep her mind off the return visit of Wild's men.

And here was the question that disturbed me: should I try to help Frenchy, or should I leave him to his fate at the hands of Wild's men?

I paced up and down, reasoning first this way and then that.

To begin, I had had a long association with Claude Delamere. We had laughed together and I could not help but be a little impressed with his way of stealing a lady's heart along with her favourite ring. Here was a man who risked much and lived life to the full, with a joke, a smile and a courtly French bow.

And yet, he had set himself against Thomas Wild and made a plan so daring that it would reach through society from the bottom to the very top, dragging down felons and noblemen alike. And he had included me, Charley Feather, in that plan without so much as a by-your-leave, so that now I was forced to flee the city of my birth (so far as I knew it) and every friendly face I had ever known.

'Charlotte, I must seek physic and a poultice from the doctor,' my mistress called at about the time in the afternoon when I boiled water in the kettle and made her tea.

'What ails you?' I asked, pretending ignorance of the morning visit.

'I have a bruising and swelling on my ribs where . . . I tripped and fell,' she replied uneasily, resting an arm across the place and moving stiffly. 'Mind the shop and don't let in any strangers.' With that she left me alone to my thoughts.

What should I do? Stand by and let Frenchy meet his fate at the hands of Wild's men? Or by some indirect means let him know of the fresh danger he was in?

I was stretched on the rack as the hands of the clock in my mistress's bedroom ticked down through the floorboards into the shop below.

I pictured Frenchy's handsome face bloodied by the fists of the bald-headed man, of his ribs broken, of wounds and cries too terrible to describe. And I thought to myself of Delamere's last words before they killed him, his final desperate pleas to Wild; how he might lie and claim that it wasn't he, but Charley Feather, who had stolen Hind's saddlebag, and that Wild had sought the wrong man all these weeks.

Was the Frenchman capable of such deceit? Certainly, without the shadow of a doubt, if it helped to save his own skin.

And so I found that there was no such thing as simply walking away from a sinful life, and that I must save Frenchy partly to save myself, with action to be taken before I set myself back on the road.

My mistress was not present when I 'sold' the gold locket I had kept about me all this time. By which I mean I left the necklace in the leather bag under her bed where she kept her gold sovereigns and took it upon myself to value the item at three of those coins, which I pocketed in a plain calico purse strung about my neck.

With money thus secure, I took bread and meat from the kitchen and left Ludgate Hill before my mistress, as I shall call her for the last time, returned.

I went from there to Paternoster Row, intending to seek out Matthew Bayes at the Green Man and warn him that if he knew the whereabouts of Claude Delamere, then he should tell his friend to remove himself from his present lodgings and give up any plan he might still cling to of opposing Wild and making his fortune.

This was as much as I could do to save my sometime friend. And more than I should have done, as it turned out.

'What do you want with Matthew Bayes?' the landlord at the Green Man inquired. He was a small, slight, plain-looking man with a quiet voice that showed he had not been born in these parts, but somewhere in the north of the country.

I glanced all about me, making sure that on this occasion there was no sign of Mary Brazier or Patrick O'Neill. 'My business is my own,' I replied. 'I only ask if you know the whereabouts of Bayes.'

'And if I do and go to fetch him, who shall I say is asking for him?' the landlord said.

'I shall not give you my name, neither,' I said proudly, 'only that the business is important and might save a friend from the hands of one who wants him dead.'

'Then you may speak to me,' the man behind the counter went on, 'for I am Matthew Bayes.'

I nodded, still anxious to keep my voice down, lest the one or two sullen drinkers in the corners of the inn overhear our conversation. 'You are to give a message to Claude Delamere,' I whispered.

Bayes's eyes narrowed. He beckoned me through to a small, shuttered room with a bare table and two low benches. Only then would he let me continue.

'Tell Frenchy that Wild's men will soon discover his lodging,' I said, uncomfortable in the close, dark room. 'Someone has betrayed him.'

'Give me names,' Bayes insisted. 'Yours and the traitor's.'

'No. I have come with a simple message. Frenchy must leave the place where he is now, and he must do this before the evening is over.'

'How will he know to trust you?' the landlord demanded, his back to the door where we had entered.

This seemed a fair question, and yet I would not give away more information to Bayes. And so, seeing a knife in a leather case attached to his belt, I leaned forward and withdrew the blade, swiftly slicing off a small lock of my red-gold hair, which I handed to the landlord along with his knife. 'Show him this,' I urged. 'This will convince him. And believe me, the case is serious!'

My action seemed to satisfy Bayes, who then opened the door and let me exit.

I made good my escape and took to the street, heading now towards Aldgate with a new and hastily formed plan, since the coach to Oxford might prove dangerous. For Wild's men on the lookout for Frenchy would surely learn who travelled between cities, so that my better chance was to secure a horse with the money I had in my pocket, and thus ride secretly out of town.

Aldgate was the place where I had deserted my poor mare, Guinevere, given freely into the care of some new master or mistress, and I hoped I might soon find her again and pay a fair price to have her back with me.

And yet I felt uneasy as I sped through the streets. I had risked much by returning to the Green Man and could not help but feel that O'Neill's presence on the last occasion had tainted the inn – a stain which I seemed to carry with me now on my clothes and skin.

Let me be free of this place! I said to myself. Of the deep, dark shadows and filthy gutters, of whispers and cold stares, of brutal men who would slit my throat and turncoats who would sell their grandmothers for a pint of ale.

At last I gained the street where I had stolen linen from the line and deserted my mare. The sun had gone down, but the day was still warm when I entered the coach-house where I hoped to find Guinevere safely stalled.

I was disappointed, however, finding only a pair of chestnut geldings there, eating hay, and I had to retreat when a groom came into the yard and shooed me away.

My sudden exit brought me face to face with a child who had followed me from the bottom of the street, who fled now on bare legs, his tattered shirt billowing behind him. What had scared him? I wondered.

A gate to a nearby yard swung and banged shut. Two women peered down at me from an upstairs window. The lad disappeared around the corner.

And then three men vaulted a wall and ran at me. One threw his arms around my arms and waist before I had chance to resist, a second gagged my mouth with a piece of filthy cloth, the third roughly pulled a sack over my head.

I felt myself pinned down, blindfolded, swept up and carried away. I kicked with my feet, tried to twist in the men's grasp, but the sack almost suffocated me and the gag bit deep into my skin.

And my dream of escape became a nightmare of rough hands and musty hessian, a tide of dark secrets, deep as the river, all rushing me helpless into the unknown.

Eleven

My kidnappers reveal themselves, whereupon I suffer the greatest shock. A plain-spoken Yorkshireman holds my life in his hands and reintroduces me to yet another old friend.

I stopped struggling at last.

My hands were tied behind my back, I was set on my feet and the sacking was removed from my head.

And so I found myself back whence I had come – in the small, private room to one side of the Green Man, staring into the face of Matthew Bayes. His two accomplices stood to either side, one an African with skin as dark as peat and a gold ring in his ear, the other a lad of some fifteen or so years.

Drawing air into my lungs and recovering from my fright, I shook my head fiercely to have the gag removed from my mouth. Even now I was looking about me for a means of escape.

'Not yet,' Bayes said, studying me with a puzzled

frown. 'You must stay a while. Ambrose, go and tell our friend that we have taken the girl.'

The African went away, leaving the youth and the landlord to stand guard. Then the youth came close and began to prod me and to lift my skirt for a glimpse of my ankle, at which I kicked him hard.

'That will teach you not to insult a lady, Daniel!' Bayes laughed, as the lad howled and hopped backwards.

'She's no lady,' said Daniel. 'She's Charley Feather!'

I drew breath again and mumbled through my gag.

Bayes walked around me, shaking his head. ' 'Tis a good disguise,' he said slowly. 'See the smoothness of his cheek, the slope of his shoulders, the narrowness of his waist . . .'

I kicked out again, but this time missed my target, for Matthew Bayes sidestepped, then told Daniel to remove my gag, for he would hear what I had to say.

'I say you are a treacherous villain!' I cried as soon as the cloth was removed. 'I came as a friend with a fair warning for Delamere, and you reward me with this!'

'Are you, or are you not Charley Feather?' Bayes demanded. 'This lock of hair I hold in my hand tells me that you are he, though the petticoats tell a different story.'

I held up my head and gave my haughtiest stare, which was interrupted by the speedy return of Ambrose and a companion. The second man stayed in the shadows, while Ambrose came up and muttered in Bayes's ear.

'Come, Daniel.' The landlord ordered the youth out, leaving the African, myself and the newcomer standing in the close, shuttered room.

I had a thought to rush after Bayes, but Ambrose spotted my intention and swiftly stood in my way. This made me step sideways, into the path of the new man, who started to speak for the first time.

'Charley Feather!' he exclaimed in the broadest of Yorkshire voices. 'Why, my lad, I would scarcely have known thee!'

I started, blinked, then stared anew at the Yorkshireman.

'Aye, 'tis a fair disguise!' He grinned. 'The skirt, the petticoats, the golden red curls!'

The Yorkshireman stood some six feet tall. His hair was short and dark, his face clean-shaven and handsome. He wore a plain, drab coat and a coarse brown waistcoat, heavily belted, with a pistol thrust through it. The pistol was a fine silver one, carved and engraved, and it was this that I recognised.

'Frenchy?' I asked, my voice high and wavering.

'Shar-lee?' he mockingly returned.

'Frenchy!' I cried again, doubting my own senses. Where were the fine lace collar and cuffs, the silk embroidered waistcoat, the flowing dark curls? Where, above all, were the courtly French manners and soft, musical, foreign voice?

'Matthew told me I would find you changed,' Delamere laughed. 'At first I did not believe it could be you, Charley!'

'And so say I. What game are *you* playing?' I demanded angrily, though my hands were still tied and I was under Ambrose's steady gaze. 'What has happened to your voice?'

'*Ah, pardon mademoiselle!*' he mocked, then reverted to his Yorkshire speech. 'It grieves me to disappoint you, Charley, my boy, but despite the reputation I have built up, there's not one drop of true French blood running through my entire body!'

'Not French!' I cried, my mouth hanging open. 'But you have noble connections, you gambled away your fortune, you escaped Madame Guillotine!'

'And you, my lad!' he retorted, ignoring my astonishment. 'What became of your boy's breeches and your fine feathered hat?'

I gave him no answer, shocked as I was by Frenchy's new guise, for a more plain and ordinary country bumpkin come down to the great city you could not hope to find.

'Don't come near me!' I warned, as he threatened to approach and settle the doubt over my gender for himself. 'I own freely that I am no more a boy than you are a Frenchman!'

'Aha!' Frenchy cried, 'the two of us have deceived the world, eh, Charley!'

'We have!' I agreed.

We stood a while to consider what we had just learned. Now that the truth was out, however, Frenchy readily volunteered all the facts.

'I am no Frenchman, but was born George Monkman, the son of a coachman on an estate near Beverley in the North Riding, and served my time as a foot soldier in my youth.'

'Villain!' I interjected.

He grinned. 'I kept bad company and fell into temptation in Flanders, where I fled my regiment for France.'

'And picked up fancy French ways,' I put in, 'and made a false life for yourself.' My head was still reeling from these discoveries.

'Aye, and I found I had a passion for fine clothes and wine, but I could not get me a rich wife, Charley, though I tried in Paris, until my story was discovered and I was forced back to London and into the company of Thomas Wild – and so you know all the rest.'

'And now you have betrayed me, Frenchy, when all my concern was to help you!' I cursed my own good intentions and regretted that I had not hastened to find myself a horse and so be on my way to Oxford.

'You're a fine one to talk of betrayal,' he countered, coming close in spite of my objection and snatching the small purse from around my neck, checking its contents and pocketing the three precious gold coins for himself.

And I thought of all the gallantry and fine phrases he had used to rob ladies on the highway, and I knew then that I preferred the Frenchy of old to this rough-hewn Yorkshireman.

'You ran from me, Charley, with a secret in your bosom. A secret that only you and I know, which is worth a king's ransom!'

'I have told no one!' I assured him, clenching my teeth so as not to let my lips tremble.

His eyes narrowed and he continued heartlessly. 'Aye, and perhaps we should cut out your tongue to make sure that you do not.'

My heart shuddered, but I did not show my fear.

'Or perhaps we should weigh you down with rocks and drown you in the river, and so be done with it,' my tormentor argued. 'For I, too, have kept the great secret close to my chest, Charley – biding my time until Wild's men have lost the scent, and then I will spring back with the contents of that letter and ruin the men who have hounded me and made my life a misery.'

'I will not tell,' I said, as proud as I could.

'Until Wild's men capture you and torture you,' Frenchy put in, leaning in close to my face, his dark eyes glittering. 'And then they will winkle the truth from those pretty lips, and I will be a dead man!'

In the corner, Ambrose stood, arms crossed, nodding his head so that the ring in his ear glinted.

'Let me go!' I pleaded, turning as soft and feminine as I was able. 'I was on my way out of this town when your men took me. I promise, Frenchy, that you will never see my face again!'

Then Frenchy sighed and said he was sorry. 'I have need of you, Charley. There are letters I must write, and I cannot shape my words. You must do it for me.'

Yes, I thought, recalling Frenchy's complaints about the 'damned, cramped' hand on the envelope and on the reward notices pinned to the trees. Delamere had been clever at hiding his ignorance, but in truth he was a mere coachman's son without an ounce of learning to his name. Fake and fraudster, George Monkman had made himself a life that was nothing more than a hollow shell.

Then I laughed at myself: for what was I if not a fraudster who had turned myself from girl to boy and back to girl again, who had hidden every true feeling I had ever experienced, and dealt double with the world for as long as I could walk on my own two feet and mouth a false sentence with my childish tongue?

'Come!' Frenchy said, ordering Ambrose to produce the sack and place it back over my head.

Then the African picked me up with ease and put me over his shoulder, and so I was conveyed down Paternoster Row like cargo from a tall ship being unloaded on to the wharf.

It was impossible to know where they took me.

I felt that they carried me down narrow streets, away from the hustle and bustle of the wide thoroughfares. Once or twice, a passer-by stopped to ask our business, it striking them as odd for a girl to be carried blindfolded and like a sack of grain across an African's shoulder. But Frenchy gave them a curt reply in a growling voice, and perhaps the strange sight of the tall African in his frock-coat and high collar was enough in itself to send them about their business.

In any case, we arrived at our destination within a few minutes, and I was set upon the ground and shoved – my eyes still covered – through a narrow doorway and down six or seven steps into what smelled like a damp cellar.

'Welcome to my den!' Frenchy declared, whipping off the sack and finally hacking the rope from my wrists with a sharp knife.

I blinked and opened my eyes. My first thought was that there was no Sara Wheeler here, to banish the spiders and whisk away the dust. The place was cavernous, grey and dingy; the brick walls laced with cobwebs. Then I took in a long, rough table littered with scraps of bread and meat, a shabby curtain strung across the entrance to an inner room and a mess of cinders in a small grate.

'Home sweet home!' Frenchy laughed, bidding Ambrose go for ale and taking off his own coat and sitting in his shirtsleeves at the table.

'Where am I?' I asked, feeling like a mole under the earth. The only light in the cellar came from a single candle set on a shelf by the dead fire.

'In the dark underbelly of this monstrous city,' Frenchy replied in a whisper, seeing that I was afraid and thus set on making me shake. 'With the rats and the starving curs, where good men never stray!'

'They will find you!' I told him. 'There is no corner where Wild's reach does not stretch.'

Frenchy laughed quietly. 'They seek a Frenchman with his "*pardons*" and "*mesdemoiselles*". But like you, Charley, I thought it best to throw them off the track. Do not look so down-in-the-mouth. We have been in better lodgings, I admit, but never in such good company.'

I frowned. *Ambrose?* He hardly seemed like a man to raise my spirits, standing silent as he did for the most part, and equally silently going off on his errands.

'Ambrose is a good man,' Frenchy asserted. 'And I would stake my life on him. But no, I did not mean the African. Why, only yesterday I was joined by someone you will be glad to see, who is even now fast asleep behind yon curtain.'

I stiffened. Was this Frenchy's idea of a joke, to frighten me with fresh accomplices who would spring out from the inner room, bind me anew and carry me off to a still darker, damper place?

'Trust me,' Frenchy urged. 'You will be pleased to meet your old acquaintance.'

And I thought, in that instant, how there were only two people in this world who would fit this description: one was in America, and the other I had recently spurned on the bank of the River Thames.

'Come!' Frenchy whispered, leading me across the great open cellar and drawing back the curtain.

And there, on a straw mattress on the floor, lay the curled figure of Mary Brazier, and next to her the huddled shape of the girl called Hannah who I had first seen at the Green Man.

'Wake up, Mary!' Frenchy cried, stooping to shake her roughly by the arm. 'We have a visitor. Come, rub your eyes and rise. Here is Charley Feather to see us, and he has a story to tell that surpasses any you have ever heard!'

I saw Mary, who gasped at the sight of me, and I

almost wept. Her poor face was cut and bruised, her clothes torn. And there was a hunted look in her once bright eyes and a manner of cowering back against the filthy wall that set my heart thumping.

'O'Neill did this,' she said grimly, as I took in the swelling over her eye and the raw graze on her cheek. 'My husband has a gentle way with him, does he not?'

'Oh, Mary!'

'Tut, these bruises will mend,' she said briskly, standing up and taking the child Hannah by the hand. 'I am a grown woman and chose him of my own free will, more fool me. But when he began on the girl here – raised his fists to her and flung her to the floor and kicked her – then I would have no more of it!'

Hannah clung to Mary, her eyes cast down, her fair hair falling forward to hide her face.

I shook my head. Where was my reckless, bold Mary of old who had thrust me out of the window of the Blue Boar in York and so secured my freedom while she herself was taken?

'O'Neill was never any friend of mine!' I declared. 'You are well rid of the brute!'

Sighing and moving stiffly out of the small chamber into the big cellar, Mary told me how she had escaped with the girl when her husband was out meeting with Thomas Wild. 'The two are very close,' she confided.

'Wild employs Patrick to keep his ear to the ground and to twist secrets out of his enemies.'

'Don't!' I could all too easily imagine the half-hanged man's methods.

'Why, Charley!' Mary gave me one of her old, bright smiles. 'You are grown timid in your girl's gown. I say "Charley", but perhaps you have a new name?'

'No, I am Charley still,' I replied stiffly, ready for more teasing from Mary.

'A wench!' Frenchy cut in with an abrupt laugh. 'And growing to be a comely one, eh, Mary?'

'You're a sly fox, Charley!' Mary said with her old merry look, 'to live with me these three years and never give away your secret. What became of the fine feathered hat and the lithe leap into the saddle?'

'Vanished,' I replied forlornly. At this moment my joyous days on the open highways seemed a mere dream. 'Gone, along with my freedom. Tell me, Mary, what is to become of me now?'

'Why, Frenchy will look after you! He has taken you in, has he not? Just as he welcomed me and the child when I let it be known that I had fled from O'Neill.'

'No, Mary, he has kidnapped me,' I countered. 'I was seized by three of his men and carried here!'

She looked at Frenchy, whose stern face confirmed the truth of my story.

'I have a use for Charley,' he said, taking the beer that

Ambrose had just brought in and pouring it into one of the pewter mugs littering the table. 'She is to write a letter whose contents will make my fortune. Meanwhile, you are to make sure she does not stray.'

'I am to be her gaoler?' Mary inquired with a puzzled frown.

Frenchy laughed and said yes, that it was her duty not to let me out of her sight, otherwise he would set O'Neill on her trail and so she and the girl would be returned to a life of misery.

Whether he spoke in earnest or not, mention of this turned Mary silent, and while Frenchy drank himself to sleep at the table, she and Hannah slipped back behind the curtain, where I followed them and we huddled together for a while.

'I would never have thought to find us in this sorry state,' Mary whispered when we heard Frenchy's snores.

'Well, I am glad to see you,' I confided, noting always that Hannah stayed close to Mary, either holding her by the hand or snuggling at her side. 'I have missed you, Mary, ever since the day they hanged Turpin and our lives took a turn for the worse. Was it hard to lie in prison in York? Did you fear for your life?'

'Aye, I thought I had my date with the hangman, Charley. But it was not so hard in the event, for Wild entertained visitors and they brought him gifts of food and ale which he shared amongst the prisoners, and so made friends with every man there, including those who held us.

'And we were not there above three days before they moved us, intending to bring us to London, but a gang of armed and masked men surprised the prison wagon, shot our guards dead and carried us to freedom.'

I nodded. 'The news was spread abroad and did not please Frenchy. But it warmed my heart to hear that you had cheated the noose.'

'God bless you, Charley, you have a soft heart.' Mary leaned closer and lowered her voice still further. 'What is Frenchy's game? What did Hind's saddlebag contain that has set Wild after him? Come, Charley, you may tell me!'

'No, I cannot!'

'Charley, I will not let our old friend Frenchy harm you.'

Still silence from me, while the child hung on to Mary's hand and stared at me with wary eyes.

'We are in this together,' Mary whispered, her voice as earnest as ever had heard it. 'We are all fugitives from Wild!'

I stared at Mary's bruised face and saw only openness and friendship there, but still I could not let go of my secret. 'It is too dangerous,' I told her, as I had once told Robert.

How could a simple letter, as light as a feather, mere

words upon the page, weigh so heavily on my shoulders? How could it have brought me to this low state?

'Tell me!' Mary urged.

But I drew back the curtain to reveal Frenchy stirring from his slumped position at the table. And, not three feet from us, standing quiet guard and listening to our every word, was the tall, dark figure of Ambrose.

Twelve

In which we flit from place to place. I put pen to paper to address the noblest in the land. There is a brawl, during which the reader will see urgent need for the introduction of law and order to the streets of London. My own circumstances do not change for the better.

'They have found a body!'

One of my kidnappers arrived at Frenchy's den with the day's news. It was Daniel, the lad who had tried to prod and poke me to prove that I could not be Charley Feather. Now he flung his hat down on the dusty table and delivered the gruesome details.

It was during the second morning I had spent in the musty cellar, after a scant breakfast of bread and cheese.

'What body? Where?' Frenchy grunted. Unshaven and still unsteady on his feet after a night spent drinking at the Green Man, my once dandyish highwayman looked grey and ill.

'An old woman. They dragged her out of the river at

low tide. She was weighted down with stones, her hands and feet were tied.'

At this I felt my blood run cold.

'Why should anyone want to murder a harmless old woman?' Mary wondered, as she and Hannah made an effort to clear the untidy table. The little girl followed in her protector's footsteps, never letting her out of her sight, even for a second.

'They say she lived on Ludgate Hill,' our informant went on. 'It turns out she dealt in silver and gold, but when they went to her shop they found it empty of all plate and jewels, so the ones that killed her did it for the money.'

I gasped and Mary noticed my shock.

'Aye well, a fence in stolen goods seldom dies in her bed,' Frenchy observed sullenly, unmoved by the death of a greedy old woman.

'Charley?' Mary inquired, putting a hand on my shoulder.

'Her name was Sara Wheeler,' I muttered, with a dry lump in my throat that made it hard to breathe. 'She was my mistress.'

At this Frenchy looked up sharply. He leaned across, tipped over my stool and pinned me against the wall. 'Say more!'

The picture of Sara trussed and drowned and cast up on the muddy bank filled my head. 'Wild's men came to the shop.' I stammered out everything I knew. 'That is why I sought you out, to warn you.'

Frenchy climbed on to the table and squatted over me. 'What did the men want?'

'My mistress was bent on betraying you. She said she knew where you hid.'

Now Frenchy hoisted me off my feet and swung me into a corner.

'Wait. I did not inform against you. How could I? I was ignorant of this place!'

'Frenchy, I believe her,' Mary said, restraining him as best she could.

Daniel and Ambrose stood on one side, watching every movement.

'Rumours run around the city like wildfire. Sara had heard one of them. She promised to pass it on to Wild for one hundred guineas.' I spoke fast, anxious to escape from the cobwebs clinging to my face and neck. 'I heard them say that once she had passed on the information, they would cut out her tongue, or else drown her in the Thames!'

Frenchy nodded and let me sink to the floor.

There was consternation in the room then, and a swift gathering up of items. Ambrose went out on to the street as lookout, reported that our way was clear, and then we left that spider-infested cellar like rats leaving a sinking ship.

* * *

We found fresh refuge in a room above Matthew Bayes's inn, and we stayed there only one day, then went at dead of night to Amen Court, where we sought shelter in an attic chamber with a sloping ceiling and view of the great dome of St Paul's – we being myself, Frenchy, Mary and Hannah, together with the African.

The rooms below us were empty, and on the ground floor there was a busy coffee house, whose rich aroma filtered up the staircase to our attic room.

'Why do you stay with Frenchy?' I asked Mary when my captor's back was turned. 'Why not strike out on your own, go to another town, begin again?'

Mary smiled for a moment. 'Away from London, yes!' she said, her eyes lighting up.

And from O'Neill and his heavy fists, I thought, wondering what it was that held her here.

And then Frenchy came swaggering back into the room, put his arm around Mary's waist and whispered into her ear. She blushed and hung her head, and I saw a shadow of the old Mary, her waist laced tight, her chestnut brown hair hanging in shining curls on her white bosom, her eyes laughing. This was the answer to my question. I was disappointed in her, and Mary saw it.

'Don't judge me,' she said later. 'I must take care of this child, whose mother died of a fever and begged me with her last breath not to desert the girl. Besides, Frenchy is not at heart a cruel man . . .'

I shook my head as her voice dwindled and she let out a great sigh.

'Write me this letter,' Frenchy demanded, putting pen and paper on the table before me.

Mary and Hannah sat in a shaft of sunlight on the far side of the high attic room. Ambrose, for once, was absent.

' "My Lord Duke," ' Frenchy dictated in an important voice, striding to the narrow window and staring out. 'Is that how you address the Duke of Newcastle?' he mused. 'Yes, begin with "My Lord Duke", Charley. Come, put the words on the paper!'

I knitted my brow and dipped the quill in the ink. Slowly, I began to write.

' "Let it be clear that your plan to pardon the felon, Thomas Wild, in return for certain information, is no longer a secret." '

At which Mary jumped to her feet and began to walk agitatedly around the bare room.

I wrote on, trying not to let my hand shake, though the letters looked spidery and awkward, not smooth and flowing as is a real secretary's hand.

' "Sir, your secret being out, this correspondent desires an immediate meeting with your Lordship, at your Lordship's convenience, and begs to point out . . ." '

'What is after "meeting"?' I asked, finding that Frenchy ran ahead and mixing up 'my lordships' in my head.

He repeated the phrase, then continued. ' "And begs to point out that the matter would prove of great interest to other members of parliament in His Majesty's opposition party, who might use it against you . . ." '

Mary gasped and her step gathered pace.

' "Prove of great interest." ' I laboured over the words Frenchy gave me.

'This cannot be!' Mary cried. 'This is treason, Frenchy. You mean to bribe a great nobleman!'

'A duke is a man like any other,' he argued. 'He has his weaknesses. Why should I not take the money of a duke, as well as that of a gentleman or a country vicar?'

'You mean to betray Wild!'

'Aye, to be sure.'

'They will hang you for your pains!' Mary was beside herself, wringing her hands and then trying to snatch the paper from the table.

Frenchy prevented her. 'If I do nothing, Wild will kill me,' he pointed out. 'If, on the other hand, the Duke of Newcastle pays me ten thousand guineas . . .'

'Ten thousand!'

'. . . If he pays me the sum I demand and withdraws

Wild's pardon, then the magistrate's men swoop to arrest my enemy and my fortune is made! You will stay by my side, dress in silks and satins, wear pearls and be admired throughout the land!'

Mary frowned and fell silent. And so she succumbed to the promise of jewels and finery, and to the quicksand promise of an out and out villain.

'. . . "Who might use it against you",' I prompted.

' "And bring you down," ' Frenchy concluded. 'Thus are mighty men destroyed by corruption,' he commented smugly. 'Charley, you will finish the letter by telling the noble duke that my messenger will await his reply and not return until he carries it in his hand – a day, a time, a place for the meeting, and so on. You will leave it unsigned, and say merely, "A faithful servant of His Majesty", and so it is done!'

The letter was written, the ink dried and the envelope sealed with wax. It was the time for action.

On the same August morning that Ambrose conveyed the letter to the Westminster office of the Duke of Newcastle, Frenchy secretly invited Thomas Heath and William Plommer to the coffee house below our lodging.

The two men came up from Southwark, across the busy river by boat, late in the evening as the sun cast a red glow on the sluggish water. The boatman led them by back ways to St Paul's and thence to Amen Court, where Frenchy – got up in his old garb of satin and lace – sat drinking coffee and smoking a pipe; for all the world as if this was a night like any other, where gentlemen would talk pleasantries over a game of cards before retiring for a sound night's sleep.

Heath and Plommer strode into the coffee house and the room fell silent.

I took in the appearance of these great gang leaders – the men whose lawless grasp spread far south of the river into the counties of Surrey and Kent, where they robbed and forged, stabbed and shot, lied and threatened, and had any man killed who stood in their way.

And yet they looked respectable enough in their powdered wigs and embroidered waistcoats, their fine tailored coats and smooth silk stockings. Two rich merchants, you would have said, with houses on the Strand and small country estates in Northamptonshire.

My fingers itched when I saw the heavy watch-chain adorning Plommer's broad chest and the pretty silver snuff-box which Heath drew out of his pocket, but I chastised myself for my old ways and stayed back in the shadows, guarded as I was by Ambrose.

It was Plommer, the smaller and slighter of the two, who first spotted Frenchy stirring his coffee with a silver spoon. He went across, took off his hat and gave a shallow bow. 'If you have brought us here on a fool's errand, I will slit your throat!' he hissed.

Heath, a man of more than six feet, lean and lithe, stood by Plommer. Neither sat down.

And I had to admire Frenchy, who did not shrink or tremble under the threat, but stood up and assured Plommer in his most courteous and 'Frenchified' voice that this was no game but, on the contrary, the most urgent of matters, concerning the future of every felon from Mayfair to Shoreditch, and south of the river all the way to the white cliffs of Dover.

Thomas Heath sat down then and sprinkled a pinch of snuff on to the back of his large hand. He breathed it into his nostril with a loud sniff. 'We may slit your throat in any case,' he warned Frenchy.

'Aye, on Wild's orders!' Frenchy commented sneeringly. 'But when you hear what I have to say, it is *his* throat you will want to slice, believe me!'

Plommer took his place by Heath, facing Frenchy across the small, polished table. 'You talk like a madman, Delamere. You know that to speak thus of the most powerful man in London is to sign your own death warrant.'

Frenchy smiled thinly. 'You knew Wild's father, Jonathan, did you not?' he asked Plommer.

The older man nodded. 'What of it?'

Frenchy leaned forward and lowered his voice. 'How did Jonathan Wild deal with betrayal?'

At this, Plommer simply raised his hand to his throat with a cutting motion. 'He had a heart of stone. None dared betray him.'

'And you suppose that his son is the same?' Frenchy's eyes darted from Plommer to Heath and back again. 'A man who rules by fear. But what if Thomas Wild himself were to turn to treachery?'

Heath sniffed again, then cleared his throat. 'Aye, this is a madman talking,' he said to Plommer, easing his tall frame upright, and flicking back the skirts of his coat to reveal a brace of pistols.

At my side, I saw Ambrose take a long knife from his belt and quietly move towards Heath.

'How would Wild betray us?' Plommer demanded, his voice still low and even. 'What would he gain?'

'Ah, now I see I have set you thinking, Mr Plommer!' Frenchy declared, noting that Ambrose had moved in on Heath. 'Suppose that there is much to gain. Say, for example, that there are powerful men in the government promising Wild a free pardon for all his felonies in return for information about you and your friend here . . .'

'Seal your lips, you scoundrel!' Heath snarled, drawing his pistol until Ambrose sprang from behind and set his knife to Heath's throat.

'Can this be true?' Plommer demanded, his brow creased.

'As true as I live,' Frenchy swore. 'Wild will have you all hanged before the summer is out!'

'Do not listen to the villain!' Heath argued, struggling with Ambrose, who drew blood and so quietened the man.

'Give me proof,' Plommer insisted.

I watched as Frenchy withdrew a paper from his pocket. He beckoned me from my corner. 'Read for me, Charley,' he commanded.

Curse the day that I was taught my letters by my foster mother! I thought to myself, dragging my heels until a fellow I did not know seized me and pushed me forward.

'Begin!' Frenchy said.

My voice faltered as I commenced. ' "Sir, it has come to the attention of His Majesty's government . . ." '

'His Majesty's government!' Frenchy repeated, raising his eyebrow and tapping the paper. 'Mark that!'

Plommer fixed Frenchy with an icy gaze while I proceeded.

' ". . . Neither can we allow a situation in our capital city . . ." '

'Faster!' Frenchy demanded.

' ". . . fellows who are known to be thieves . . . shall defy the laws and laugh at justice." ' I trembled as I spoke.

'Now slower!' Frenchy told me as I approached the nub of the matter.

' "And so I am empowered, as Secretary of State—" '

'Secretary of State!' Frenchy declared, tapping again.

' ". . . to offer a pardon to you, Thomas Wild, for all crimes whatsoever committed by you, on whomsoever, whether, in town or country, through all the length of this land." '

'Proof enough, Plommer?' Frenchy asked with a smile.

At which Heath broke free from Ambrose and lunged at Frenchy, until several fellows set upon him and demanded to hear out the conclusion of the letter, which Frenchy grasped from my hand and recited the final words, as though they were engraved on his heart.

' "The pardon to hold good so long as the said Thomas Wild promised to discover each and every one of his agents and apprentices so the State may try and execute these same felons . . ." '

There was confusion then as William Plommer sprang up in an attempt to seize the letter, but Frenchy withdrew it and held it, by accident, close to Heath, whose blood dropped on to the white paper and spattered it with scarlet – at which Frenchy swore in his Yorkshire tongue and surprised all who were gathered, giving Ambrose the opportunity to restore his hold on

Heath while others disarmed the villain and then surrounded Plommer.

Cornered, Heath nodded. 'You win, Frenchy. You have convinced me that there is a plot afoot and my neck is at risk.'

'And this letter is the reason why Wild would have me killed!' Frenchy declared, waving the blood-stained paper in the air. 'Why I have lived like a rat in the gutter these past weeks, while you and your men hunted me down!'

Heath nodded again. 'Give me the letter,' he urged Frenchy slyly. 'With it, I can turn every villain in the city against your sworn enemy.'

But Frenchy laughed and restored the paper to his breast pocket. 'Forgive me, but I will keep it safe, lest it fall into the wrong hands!'

So Heath and Plommer had to make do with what they had heard. While Plommer stemmed the flow of blood from his neck with a handkerchief, the other gang leader wrested himself free from the rough grasp of the crowd.

'Thomas Wild is a dead man!' someone muttered, judging the look of rage on the two villains' faces.

'Aye, he will not see the morning!' another guessed.

But I foresaw that not everyone there was in agreement, and noted an old fellow slip out unseen, no doubt foreseeing a weighty reward that would land in his lap if he were the first to seek out Thomas Wild to warn him what had passed.

And so I conclude that there is no honour among thieves, as the saying is, and I expect more than William Plommer's blood to be shed before the sun rises again over the great dome of St Paul's.

Thirteen

A second brief episode which the more squeamish among you may wish to overlook.

It was thick night when Heath and Plommer departed from the coffee house and Ambrose carried me back up the stairs to Mary and Hannah.

'Charley, where is Frenchy? What has happened?' Mary cried, rushing to me and sitting me down in the sole chair by the window, so that she could see me by the light of the moon.

'Frenchy is safe,' I assured her, 'but there is much ado. I would I were not here to witness it, Mary.'

She gathered Hannah to her. 'I heard men brawling in the street,' she confessed. 'They passed around the name of Thomas Wild in the same breath as "treachery".'

'Aye, Frenchy has unleashed the dogs of civil war. Word is out and Wild's men turn against him, but there will be those who stay loyal. Blood will run in the gutters, Mary, believe me!'

My words pushed Mary into a frenzy. She turned on the African and began to plead with him to let us go free.

'Have pity,' she begged. 'The gangs of London are roused, Ambrose. I must look out for Hannah and Charley.'

'I have no need of your protection!' I argued, calculating whether or not the slope of the tiled roof outside the window was too steep for me to scale, and so take me high above the streets out of harm's way.

In any case, Ambrose proved the most vigilant of gaolers, for he bolted the door and fastened the shutter across the window.

'What is it to you?' I demanded of the African, while Mary took care of a weeping Hannah. 'Are you a lapdog to fall in with Frenchy's wishes at every end and turn?'

Ambrose did not reply.

'You have a mind of your own, do you not? Then you must see that it is nothing to release Mary and the girl? What use are they? You may keep me if you wish, for I am valuable to Frenchy, but let them go before the fighting begins!'

'I cannot,' Ambrose said.

'But you can. Simply unbolt the door. Ambrose, what is to prevent it?'

'I cannot. I will not,' came the reply.

'Hush, child!' Mary coaxed as Hannah clung to her.

'Do not leave me, Mary, as my mother left me!' the girl pleaded with a childish whine. 'Say you will not go!'

A heart of ice would have melted at the scene.

'I will not let them go because I owe my life to Delamere,' Ambrose continued in his deep, slow voice. 'I will not disobey him.'

'How do you owe him your life?' I demanded, thinking perhaps that Frenchy had rescued Ambrose from a violent brawl.

The African stood tall in the gloom. 'I escaped from a ship newly docked at Blackfriars, carrying a cargo of slaves from my home in northern Africa.'

My eyes widened and I fell silent.

'Delamere found me in chains, hiding amongst bales of cotton. The ship's captain and his men were hard on my heels.'

'Frenchy delivered you from a life of slavery?'

Ambrose nodded. 'The captain would have had me whipped to death.'

I regarded Ambrose anew. What life had he known in the north of Africa? What of his family? Was it courage or despair, or hope of returning home that had led him to break free from his slave-master?

'Hush, Hannah!' Mary urged again as she heard the heavy step of Frenchy on the stairs.

'There will be no sleep tonight!' he proclaimed as he entered the attic, his face flushed, his eyes glittering. 'A villain from the coffee house has sent word to Wild that his secret is out and that Heath and Plommer go after him as baying dogs hunt the stag. Now thieves and murderers creep out of their lairs, armed with knives, swords and pistols. Some take one side, some the other, and all gather on Watling Street.'

'How many men?' Mary gasped.

'Hundreds. The streets crawl with pickpockets and footpads. Much ale is drunk. They await orders, but they will not be contained for long.'

'Where will we hide? What will we do?' Mary cried. 'They will come for us here and drag us into the street and murder us!'

Now it was my turn to quieten the child, for fear had driven Mary out of her wits. 'We will be safe,' I promised Hannah, sounding more certain than I felt.

Hannah nodded and wiped the tears from her eyes. I felt a small hand slip into mine.

In the street below I could hear the cries of voices and the sound of many feet marching.

'Come!' Frenchy declared, swiftly throwing on his plain coat to hide his finery. 'We will not stay like rats in a trap. Let us take to the streets and lose ourselves in the crowds.'

I put a cloak around Hannah's shoulders and bid her follow, urging Mary to do the same. Soon we had joined the throng and were carried along through

St Paul's churchyard into the western end of Watling Street.

There we were met by a sight that sent a chill into my heart. Gathered on one side of the road was a band of armed villains supporting Wild. Opposite them, all carrying blades and cudgels, or whatever weapon they could lay hands on, were Heath and Plommer's men.

'Here comes Thomas Wild!' a supporter yelled as two figures on horseback galloped through the flat tombstones on to the street, where they reined in their mounts. I saw that the first was Wild and the second rider was Patrick O'Neill.

From the other direction, I made out the tall figure of Heath towering above a gang of men carrying flaming torches. Beside him stood William Plommer, in shirtsleeves now, and without his waistcoat and wig.

The noise died as the rival leaders stood face to face. Every man there waited for the order to fight, their faces shadowed, brutal hatred glittering in their eyes.

'Thomas Wild, you have delivered us to the hangman!' Plommer opened his mouth and yelled savagely. 'May you rot in hell!'

Wild gazed down from his horse, which pranced and threw its head this way and that. Wild's face showed nothing – not fear, nor anger. It was hard and passionless.

Standing close against a draper's window, I held fast

to Hannah's hand while Mary went on arguing with Frenchy.

'This is not fit for the child!' she protested. 'There will be blows, shots will be fired . . .!'

'Stay, mistress!' Frenchy insisted between gritted teeth. 'Heath and Plommer's men outnumber Wild. All will be well.' At which he gave an order to Ambrose then left our small group to seek a better vantage point for himself.

I searched up and down the street, as always looking for escape. Besides the gangs, there were many bystanders, all roused from their beds by the news that the gangs were on the march. Most were men, though some women and children were there to watch, and for a moment I thought I spotted the face of my friend, Robert Major, but when I looked again, the place where he had stood was empty, and so I believed I had imagined it.

Then Wild opened his mouth for the first time. 'Go back to your homes,' he told Heath and Plommer. 'Tomorrow we will talk.'

'Coward, there will be no more talk!' Plommer roared, seizing a torch and throwing it in a shallow arc towards Wild. It landed in a fountain of sparks at the feet of O'Neill's horse, which shied and raised itself on its hind legs.

And then Plommer gave the order for his gang to

rush forward, each man thrusting his firebrand into the faces of the enemy, while Wild sat fast in the saddle, aimed his pistol and fired.

The first shot hit Heath in the chest. He staggered and fell to the ground, dark blood oozing from the wound. I saw him struggle to raise himself to his knees, then tore my gaze away as Mary screamed in terror.

And here was O'Neill, thrusting his horse through the mob, forcing men apart until he reached Mary's side, his face dark and contorted, snarling out words of hatred against his wife.

'Mary, you are a faithless whore!' he hissed, his horse pressing her against the wall, its reins entangling her arm. As the horse raised its head, so Mary was wrenched off her feet. O'Neill leaned sideways and took her by the hair. All around, shots were fired, knives and swords flashed and men cried out in pain.

But when Ambrose saw Mary's plight, he lunged at O'Neill and with his great strength, he dragged the villain from the saddle, thrusting him under the belly of the horse so that O'Neill released his hold on Mary and fell to the ground where his own horse trampled him.

I gasped, then looked about me. Plommer's men were in the ascendant now, forcing Wild's gang back into the churchyard. Dead men and those who were badly injured lay on the bloodied ground.

And here was my chance. While Ambrose rescued

Mary from O'Neill and all was confusion, I might vanish into the darkness and so my nightmare would end. Except that Hannah gripped my hand and cried, and I had to take the child with me, down a narrow gap between two houses, leaving behind the groans of wounded men, heading away from the great church, west towards St Mary le Bow.

'Run faster!' I urged my weeping companion, my heart pounding and missing a beat at every lurking shadow, for every dark doorway might at this time conceal a murderer.

Hannah stumbled but held tight. I pitied her cries and put my arm around her, hurrying her along as best I could, across a courtyard, down an alleyway . . . and straight into Robert Major's arms!

'Come with me!' he whispered, bundling us sideways down yet another alley.

Hannah pulled back, but I overcame my surprise and urged her on. 'He is a friend,' I explained. 'He will keep us safe.'

Still she resisted, so Robert picked her up and ran with her, away from the sound of the fighting mob.

We darted between tall houses, beneath shop signs, through gateways, down a maze of strange passages populated only by rats and stray dogs, heavy with the stench of the city.

'Robert, stop!' I begged.

'No, we must hurry!' he insisted, always looking over his shoulder. 'Safety lies across the river. I will guide you.'

And I must trust him – for I had no choice, following in his footsteps as we approached the wharves, hearing the lap of the water against a wooden jetty, glimpsing the tall masts silhouetted against the moonlit sky.

'Frenchy holds me prisoner!' I told him, catching my breath as Robert carried Hannah down some steps into a small rowing boat moored between two ocean-going crafts. The ships creaked and shifted at anchor. The small boat rocked dangerously as Robert deposited his burden.

'You must tell me your story later,' he muttered. 'There is a place in Southwark where you may hide.'

And though I was afraid of the water's murky depths, I went after our saviour, feeling my foot slide on the slimy steps, so that Robert had to reach up to catch me by the waist and lift me into the unsteady boat.

As I huddled beside Hannah, Robert ran back up the steps to release the mooring rope. I was staring up at a cloud-filled sky, dreading the night passage across the river, when a man appeared above us on the gangplank of the neighbouring ship. He was aiming a pistol at Robert, warning him to stop, and I could not make him out by his appearance, for it was thick dark, but I knew the voice of Frenchy.

'Continue at your peril!' he cried to Robert, who held the rope in his hand and intended to cast us loose.

'Take the oars, Charley!' Robert yelled from the wharf, disregarding Frenchy and casting the rope into the water below. 'Row for your life!'

At which Frenchy aimed and fired his pistol. I saw Robert reel from the impact, my heart lurched, and there was a moment when I thought that Frenchy would shoot us too.

Frantic, I seized the oars, fastened them into the iron cradles and began to row, but I had not pulled above three or four clumsy strokes before Frenchy ran from the plank, back along the top deck of the sailing ship, following our progress out into the mainstream. He sprinted to the prow, poised for a moment, then plunged into the water.

Our small boat rocked, one oar slid from my grasp as our pursuer surfaced close by. His face was pale in the black water, his hand reached out to take hold of the side of the boat.

I used my second oar to beat him off, but the terrified child at my side stood up and unsteadied us further, toppling us towards Frenchy, who used his weight to bring us crashing against the low side of the boat, whence we tumbled into the cold, black depths.

I felt myself sink and the water close over my head. I could see nothing of Hannah, could feel only the icy element surround me and stop my breath. Further and further I sank, and I thought I must die a watery death, until a strong hand laid hold of me and dragged me upwards.

We burst to the surface, gasping and struggling. I could not swim and felt myself dragged helplessly through the water to the wharf, my head reeling. Then Frenchy, my rescuer, lugged me roughly on to dry land, cursing me and swearing he would never have saved me except for the use I was to him in reading and writing, and but for that he would have left me to drown.

Crouched on the stinking wharf, I began to sob. I looked to the spot where Robert had fallen but could not discover him, and then I gazed into the dark water for poor Hannah, and of her there was no sign.

Fourteen

In which the dead are counted and French manners are resumed. A summons arrives from on high, and we are dazzled by a world of wealth and splendour.

My heart ached sorely after the events of that night, and I wished that Frenchy had left me to drown indeed.

'I am to blame!' I wept in Mary's arms, my whole frame racked with sobs. 'It is as if I put my own hands around the poor child's throat and squeezed the breath out of her!'

In spite of her grief, Mary tried to soothe me. 'You could not help it,' she murmured. 'In times such as these, the innocent are harmed as well as the guilty.'

I would not be comforted, however, for I had the fresh blood of Robert Major on my hands and conscience, as well as the life of poor Hannah.

And I saw again that Hannah had been my younger self – alone and helpless in the city, prey to any cruel man or woman who might take her up and misuse her, until Mary came and took her under her wing. Hannah, with her pale, serious face and staring eyes, her small, lisping voice and clinging ways. And I had been the cause of her death.

A hollow feeling entered my soul and would not leave me. At night I dreamed of a slight body plummeting down and down through dark depths, fair hair streaming, until it reached the muddy bed and grew entangled in black weeds which wrapped themselves around the corpse and held it in a deadly embrace.

'Eat,' Ambrose urged, setting down a plate of bread and cheese before me.

Frenchy had moved us on from the attic above the coffee house to more respectable lodgings on Cheapside, which was two rooms above a tailor's shop, comfortably furnished with good chairs and soft beds. We were no longer in hiding after the defeat of Thomas Wild, but rather admired by our good neighbours for having brought about the downfall of one of the most vicious criminals in the history of the city.

For after the dreadful events which I have recounted, Wild lay in Newgate Prison, awaiting trial at the winter assizes, where he was to be indicted on a single count: namely for stealing a horse worth five pounds, this being the property of Sir Piers Checkley of Clerkenwell on the ninth day of July, 1738 – a petty enough charge which would, however, bring Wild to the gallows as well as any.

'This time there will be no escape,' Frenchy assured us, citing his own letter to the Duke of Newcastle as the reason why Wild would lie in chains until he went to the gallows. 'There will be no visitors to bring him food and drink, no jest with the gaolers, no merriment in Newgate. The reputation of His Majesty's government is at stake now, and so Wild will be made an example of and hanged.'

From this you will see that my gaoler, my kidnapper, my tormentor and erstwhile companion was well satisfied by the turn of events, except that he was nervous over the letter he had made me write to the great Duke, and would wait anxiously every day for a reply.

'Yes, Charley, you must eat.' Mary took up Ambrose's tune, when on the third day after the riot she found me sitting staring listlessly out of the window. 'Or at least drink a little of this fresh milk.'

Still I could not. I was haunted by two dead faces.

'You make yourself ill by thinking too much,' Mary murmured, laying a hand over mine. 'We cannot change what has happened.'

'But I cannot forgive myself.'

'What of Frenchy?' she asked in a lower voice still. 'Is he not to blame?'

I nodded. 'I do not forgive him either, Mary, and I wonder how you can still be his friend.'

This silenced her a while, then she spoke up. 'I do not choose to remain here, but while O'Neill lives I must stay.'

Startled, I grasped her hand. 'O'Neill is alive?' It was the first I had heard of this, and it dragged me from my grief.

'Alive in Lambeth, though his body is much broken.'

I closed my eyes and shuddered at the memory of the horse's hooves crashing down on the villain. 'He has more lives than a cat!' I breathed.

'They say he cannot walk,' Mary confided. 'He swears revenge against Frenchy, but while he lies helpless and Plommer takes control of the gangs, Frenchy says there is no need to fear him.'

And yet I did, for the very image of the man's broad, marked face, livid scars and coarse features made me shiver. And Mary was afraid too, though she did not admit it.

Strange to say, this news of O'Neill brought me round somewhat. *I must keep myself in health and able to flee*, I reckoned, in case that old enemy rose from his bed in

Lambeth and came north of the river to wreak his revenge.

So I drank a little milk, and then took bread under Ambrose and Mary's kind gaze.

Then Mary brought me fresh linen and combed my hair, which hung in long curls now. She pinned it in a pretty fashion and made me 'more womanly', as she said.

My clean appearance drew a compliment from Frenchy when he returned from a night of card playing at a fashionable salon, and then he teased me and we were in some measure back to our old manners, for Delamere had reverted to his preferred Frenchified guise under which I first knew him and the plain Yorkshireman had vanished. And few in London realised the truth, so most, again, took the dashing French villain at face value. I too played the old game, though in my heart I held a bitter anger against him for the murderer of Robert and Hannah.

'There is a date set for Wild's trial!' he announced, settling down in a chair by the fire and making room for Mary to sit beside him. 'The Grand Jury has gathered to study the indictments, has marked them as a True Bill and will bring him to trial on the thirteenth of September.'

'And that will be the end of him,' Mary said with a sigh. 'We will be at liberty to go about as we please, unless O'Neill recovers.'

'O'Neill is nothing – a broken reed – without Wild,' Frenchy assured her, his arm around her waist. 'And when we have made our bargain with my Lord Duke, we will rise above this low type of life and take a large house with servants, and employ tailors and dressmakers, grooms and coachmen, until you will not know us from true gentry, Mary!'

I thought she would protest at this and call it foolishness, but she did not. Instead she said, coyly, that she could not marry him and live as his wife while O'Neill was alive.

He stopped her mouth with a kiss. 'That is the last time that man's name is to be mentioned among us!' he declared, and she nestled close, happy to agree.

The next morning I went into the street for the first time since grief had brought me low. I had Ambrose as my companion, and I think we were a strange sight, this tall African with the ring in his ear and the slight, red-headed girl – for people looked closely and whispered amongst themselves. Or else, they knew our recent story and found it worthy of comment.

In any case, I was uncomfortable when women gossiped behind their hands and apprentices came out of shops to stare. After a while I grew hot and faint, and had to abandon my errand to buy bread, which had been Mary's excuse for sending me into the fresh air.

'I must sit down,' I said weakly to Ambrose, who found me a place outside a goldsmith's shop and promptly went inside for water.

My weak condition flustered me and drew yet more attention. A lad came up and fanned me with his leather apron. A woman with a child asked me my name.

And then, before Ambrose could return, a man in a dark, curled wig and bright-green velvet coat adorned with gold approached me. He bowed low and asked if I knew the Frenchman, Claude Delamere.

The name brought me to my senses, and I stood upright. The haughty look of the man made me curtsey, but I guarded my answer. 'Who asks after him?'

Irritated, he narrowed his eyes. 'You are not in the gutter now, mistress, with your petty suspicions and cheap impertinence. You are dealing with persons of quality, who have been watching you with interest. And so I ask you again, do you know Delamere?'

There was no time to answer, however, because Ambrose came out of the goldsmith's shop and, with a rough shove, set the man back on his heels.

My inquisitor brushed himself down. 'You know that you lay hands on the Duke of Newcastle's man, sir!' he declared angrily.

Persons of quality indeed! I might have guessed by

his way of talking, as if rolling a stone over his tongue, and by the expanse of embroidery on his coat, that this was a messenger from on high.

'Ambrose only meant to defend me from a stranger, sir,' I explained, adopting a polite speech. 'You must forgive his roughness and continue with your message, for we are indeed acquainted with the Frenchman.'

The man arched his eyebrow and looked to see if I mocked him with my change of manner. 'You will tell Delamere that the Duke received his letter,' he said stiffly. 'He has considered its contents and desires to meet with Monsieur Delamere.'

Then it was my turn to let my eyebrows rise. Here was the moment that Delamere had longed for. And yet, I was suspicious. 'How can we be sure that you come from my Lord Duke?'

Again came the narrowing of the eyes, accompanied this time by a sneering smile. But the man took a letter from his pocket and showed me a noble seal, set with the imprint of the Duke of Newcastle himself. 'You will take this to Delamere,' he ordered. 'In it is the time and the place to meet. Do not lose the letter, mistress, on pain of your life.'

I nodded and took the paper from him.

'Do not fail!' he insisted, stepping back from the shelter of the goldsmith's awning. 'The Duke is a man busy with affairs of state. He can ill afford the time.'

Aye, I think to myself, *but not too busy nor too powerful to ignore Frenchy's threat.* I said nothing, however, but curtsied and went with Ambrose on my way.

'What was the man's appearance?' Frenchy demanded the instant I had handed him the letter.

'Small, slight, with a smooth complexion and a sneering smile, but with the look and voice of a gentleman,' I replied.

'Was he accompanied?'

'No, he came alone.'

'How dressed?'

'In a coat of green velvet, with cream waistcoat, brown breeches and stockings of white silk.'

'The Duke's man, you say?' Nervously, Frenchy turned the letter over and over. 'My time has come!' he murmured to himself, as if certain that by this method of bribery he would achieve his rightful place.

Yet, even now, when Frenchy scaled the heights of society and began to meet with nobility, he needed *me*, Charley Feather.

'Read!' he commanded, thrusting the letter before my eyes.

I looked him in the eye and held his gaze. 'You will want a library when you are a great man,' I reminded him contemptuously. 'You will need to learn your letters and write your name.'

'Take heed, Charley, and cease your impudence! You forget that I know your darkest secrets!'

And would betray me to the magistrate at the drop of a hat! I thought. For though Delamere was in a good humour since the imprisonment of Wild, his kindness and gallantry were but skin deep, as we know.

As for myself, I had decided to bide my time until I could repay him in full for that dreadful night.

Three o'clock on the following afternoon was the hour set for Frenchy's assignation with Thomas Pelham-Holles, Duke of Newcastle. The place was to be a walled garden close by the south side of Westminster Abbey, which we would reach by taking a boat upstream from Blackfriars. I say 'we', for Frenchy insisted on me accompanying him, while Ambrose remained at home with Mary.

I argued against the trip, not least because it brought me close to the place where Robert had been shot and Hannah had drowned and I foresaw that this would worsen my nightmares, which continued still. But Delamere was heartless and said that he needed me in case there were letters to look over or papers to be signed.

So we had a boatman row us to our destination; a

broad, strong-armed fellow who chattered – without catching his breath – about a great cargo of spices just come in from the East Indies, or cotton from Egypt and sugar from Barbados, so that his voice floated over my head and left me to my own thoughts.

This will be my final journey with Frenchy, I promised myself. *He will make his bargain with the great Duke and then my role will be done, for what use will he have of Charley Feather when he has grasped his fortune and is living the life of a wealthy man?*

I nodded to myself, noting the huddled houses on the southern bank of the river and the great Palace of Westminster looming ahead of us to the north. And then I stared into the brown water, picturing the time, not far hence, when I would slip away from Ambrose, Mary and Frenchy and once more make my lonely way on to the highway, where I would resume my old life, unhindered.

I came to with a start.

'Make haste, Charley!' Frenchy commanded, offering me his hand as he stepped from the boat.

We had arrived at our destination and the boatman had taken his fare.

I felt my heart falter as I climbed the steps on to the wide wharf. I felt there was danger in these strange, open walkways and grand, towering buildings carved with the stone faces of dragons and devils – more so than in the filthy back streets and alleys which were my home. But Frenchy walked ahead with a confident stride, and I picked up my skirt and ran after him.

'What if the Duke plays you false?' I muttered. 'It is folly to threaten so great a man.'

'The greater the man, the further he has to fall, and so he is surrounded by fears, crowded around with corruption, plagued by doubts – in a word powerless against such as I, when I hold in my hand evidence that would condemn him in the eyes of the world.'

I shook my head at this, but knew Frenchy would not listen. We crossed a garden of quince and apple trees where fine ladies walked with their small dogs or alighted from coaches in two and threes. Beyond the garden grew a line of yew trees, spreading their low, twisted branches over an ancient wall, and it was to a narrow gate in this wall that Frenchy directed his steps.

We were met there by the man who had accosted me on the previous morning, though today he was dressed in a coat of dark blue, with a sky-blue waistcoat and breeches to match. The tresses of his curled wig were tied back by a black velvet bow.

'Come!' he urged Frenchy, without politeness, pushing us through the gate into an area some thirty yards across: an enclosed garden made up of box trees clipped into strange shapes of animals and birds, where grass was criss-crossed by walkways, and stone benches and statues of cupids were scattered here and there. In the middle was a fountain of sparkling water, falling into a round pond where golden fish swam.

Frenchy looked about him to make sure that this was no trap.

'His Lordship will speak with you for five minutes,' the lackey warned. 'There is a Bill passing through parliament this very afternoon, and serious matters which he must attend to.'

'There is no matter more serious than this,' Frenchy muttered, looking to a second gate on the far side of the garden. It opened and the man we sought came in.

The Duke of Newcastle walks like a man who knows his worth. His foot is well shod in Spanish leather, and he places it elegantly upon the ground. In one gloved hand he holds a staff tipped with silver; in the other, a handkerchief edged with lace. On his head perches a large white wig, curled across the front and hanging in ringlets to his shoulders.

Frenchy bows low and bids me curtsey.

'What have you to say to me?' the Duke asks, his voice thin and delivered down his nose. 'Come, make haste and be done!'

I do not dare look up to his face; instead I fix my gaze on the jewelled and embroidered front of the great man's striped silk waistcoat.

Frenchy draws himself up and begins. 'My Lord, you have made a bad bargain in the past that would endanger you if it were to get out . . .'

'Speak plainer, man!' the Duke snaps. 'In your letter you talk of Thomas Wild.'

'Aye, sir!'

'The villain lies in Newgate. What more do you want?'

'Aye, he rots in gaol, much against your wishes,' Frenchy challenges. The Duke has bid him speak plain and so he does. 'And I have in my possession an old letter which promised him a pardon, which will undo you, for it is signed and sealed, and can be taken before any court in this land to prove you a villain as low as Wild himself!'

'Curb your tongue!' the Duke's sky-blue lackey warns, but he is no match for Frenchy's fierce gaze.

The Duke turns and walks five or six steps from us, then returns. 'Show me the letter!'

Frenchy shakes his head. 'Upon my life, you must credit me with more wit than to bring the document with me. Only know that it is safely locked away, and if you play me false it will be brought out by others and used against you.'

'Sir, you threaten a member of His Majesty's government!' the Duke splutters, his thin face reddening with helpless rage. 'It is an act of treachery. I can have you hanged!'

'Aye, and my head displayed on Tyburn Hill!' Frenchy laughs. 'But it would not be long before yours sat alongside for the crows to peck at!'

'What would you have?' the Duke demands in a tone of cold resignation.

Frenchy allows his lips to stretch into a smile as his prize draws near. 'Ten thousand guineas,' he says in a low, calm voice.

Fifteen

*The temptations of the flesh are great and yet we see
the limits of what money can buy.*

'It is too much!' Mary gasped when I told her the sum. 'Why, we could buy half the houses in London for ten thousand guineas!'

Frenchy laughed. 'Not so much of the "we", mistress! It is I who have taken the risks, and *my* fortune, not yours.'

Aye, if it ever falls into your hands! I thought. I supposed, like Mary, that Frenchy had misjudged his man, remembering how the Duke had sworn great oaths against him and threatened to have him thrown into gaol for his wickedness, saying that he would pay the money over his own dead body.

But Frenchy walked like a man who had already achieved his goal; head up, whistling a tune, even though he had not so far received a penny piece. 'To beat a politician, you must think like one,' he asserted. 'What does the great man gain by having me thrown into

Newgate? He knows I have friends who would betray him and so bring him down in any case.'

'Then he might have you killed,' I suggested, eager to prick the bubble of Frenchy's confidence. 'One dark night, when you least expect it, a murderer may spring out and cut your throat.'

Frenchy's smile lost its brilliance. 'Mary would still speak out after I was dead, would you not?'

She frowned, then nodded.

'But she does not know where you have hidden Wild's letter,' I muttered low. 'There would be no evidence against the Duke.'

Frenchy cuffed me then for my insolence. 'His Lordship will pay within the week!' he declared. 'I will hand over the damned letter to his lackey, in return for wealth beyond our wildest dreams.'

'I will buy me a gown for morning and a gown for the evenings,' Mary decided, looking in the mirror in the room she shared with Frenchy.

I watched and listened, listlessly gazing out of the window at the grey roofs and smoke curling from the tall chimneys.

'When I rise I will put on a skirt the colour of apricots over petticoats of French lace. My bodice will be crimson, my shift of purest white cambric.' She sighed, lifting curls which rested on the back of her neck, twisting her hair into a becoming style. 'I am still young, Charley. I will wear a pearl necklace. I will go about as a lady.'

'And shall you be happy?' I inquired, my heart burdened as before.

'As happy as a princess!' she declared, clasping both hands against her bosom.

'Though you will know how Frenchy came about his fortune?' I persisted. Dreams of silk and lace did not tempt me.

My companion left off her sighing and smiling and sat me down on the bed. 'You are not to speak of that, Charley. You must be grateful. You must not spoil Frenchy's good humour.'

'And if I do?'

'Then I will not be your friend,' she said, pouting. She was silent and serious a while, then went on. 'You know what it is to be hungry, and to lie in the gutter without a roof over your head. And so do I, Charley, and I will not go back to those ways on any account. Besides, all men come by their wealth dishonestly, by treading over others and keeping them under by force. Why, for every landowner there are twenty thousand downtrodden peasants; for every merchant trading cotton there is a colony of slaves!'

There was justice in this, and so I fell silent.

'Are you not tempted?' Mary asked me more gently, stroking my cheek.

I shook my head once, then sighed. *Perhaps I am*, I thought.

'Are you certain? You would look well in a gown of softest green. It would suit your colour. We would embroider your bodice with gold.'

' 'Tis true, I would not go back to the gutter,' I admitted, feeling myself half persuaded, in spite of Robert and Hannah. 'Is this the choice we face?'

'It is, my dear.' Mary stood me up, straightened my skirt and patted my hair. 'And so, do as I do. Be a good girl, Charley, and Frenchy will take care of you.'

'The letter!' demands Sir Bernard Ainsworth, which is the name of the Duke of Newcastle's sky-blue man whom we have met twice before.

Frenchy holds the blood-stained paper aloft, as if teasing his man. 'The money first!' he retorts.

It is within the week, as Frenchy predicted. A message has come to our lodgings inviting us to attend Sir Bernard in his room behind the Palace of Westminster.

We made our way through the streets, Frenchy and I. Our path waylaid by the procession of many judges and lords into the Upper House of Parliament, with all the trumpets blaring and the heralds in their tunics of scarlet and gold.

In the parade I see the tall but stooping figure of the Duke of Newcastle himself, though of course he does not spy us in the crowd, and has handed over this murky business to his lackey. Then the King's golden coach passes by, and, though we do not have a clear view of His Majesty, all his subjects doff their hats and cry 'Hurrah!'

When the procession is over, Frenchy and I continue through a courtyard into Dean's Yard, and the meeting with Sir Bernard, who is colourfully dressed as ever, his manner foppish and disdainful.

His room is small and lined with oak, its shelves burdened with books bound in red and green. There is a wooden shield bearing a coat of arms above the fireplace.

'I will not release the letter until Charley has looked over the banker's letters,' Frenchy insists, pushing me forward to the knight's desk. 'Check the number of noughts on the documents,' he instructs me. 'Make sure they do not cheat us!'

Sir Bernard sneers but pushes the papers across the desk. 'Aye, check the noughts, Charley!' he echoes, his voice full of contempt for this villain who cannot make out his numbers.

I read them. They swim before my eyes, but I read the numeral 1, followed by four round, plump noughts, and much lettering to confirm that the Duke of Newcastle has paid over the money to Claude Delamere.

'And now, the letter!' Sir Bernard insists, nervous now that Frenchy has seized the banker's paper.

Frenchy plays with him a little. 'Down on your knees!' he demands, flicking back his coat to reveal his pistols.

Sir Bernard protests.

'Down on your knees!' Frenchy repeats, pulling out a gun with his right hand. 'Do you have a wife and children, sir?'

'Aye!' Sir Bernard says, falling to the floor, his eyes rolling from Frenchy to me to the door and back again. The sneer is gone from his face.

'And do you have an estate in the country?'

'Aye, in Northamptonshire.'

'Then we will be neighbours!' Frenchy laughs, coming in closer. 'That is, if I choose to spare your life.'

I feel my mouth go dry. I have seen too much blood of late.

'What is your fortune, sir? Is it as much as ten thousand guineas?'

'Not so large,' Sir Bernard gasps. 'Do not kill me. I merely do my master's bidding!'

'Aye, it is everyman's cry that they but follow their master's will. A murderer will say so on the step of the gallows, as well as a grand knight such as you!'

Sir Bernard hangs his head.

'Come!' I mutter to Frenchy. 'We must carry these papers to the bank.'

And so he lets the man up off his knees, but there is a final twist, as, instead of handing over Wild's tattered and stained letter, he pockets it and makes his bow. 'You must tell the Duke that Claude Delamere holds the letter in his safekeeping, as an insurance for his future well-being.'

'Liar and cheat!' Ainsworth protests, making a feeble lunge towards Frenchy, who knocks him off his feet.

Frenchy points the gun a second time, speaking slowly. 'I see you will lose your position and livelihood over this,' he confides in a mocking tone, at the same time waving the banker's documents in his face. 'But take heart, Sir Bernard. If poverty beckons and necessity forces you to dispose of your Northamptonshire property, you see before you one who has the means, and would gladly buy the estate from you, lock, stock and barrel!'

There was a night of wild celebration, when Frenchy openly returned to his old haunt, the Green Man on Paternoster Row. He bought drinks, played cards and caroused until dawn with the landlord, Matthew Bayes, the lad Daniel who had kidnapped me, Ambrose and half a dozen other footpads and highwaymen of his acquaintance.

Mary and I accompanied him, she with a flushed complexion and excited manner. I was more subdued and could not join the merriment.

'I am rich as Croesus!' Frenchy crowed, quaffing ale and leaping up on to a table. 'You see before you a man who need never take to the highway more, who has made his own good fortune even though the world was against him!'

'Aye!' his friends cried, never asking where he had made his money, but raising their tankards to toast him. 'Up with Frenchy! Down with Wild!'

I watched the drunken gang and felt a sour taste rise in my throat, onto my tongue. They were men battered by life's harshness, with limps, twisted hands and scarred faces – not a wholesome body amongst them, and they were unshaven and dirty, their hair lank.

And yet Mary laughed and raised her glass with them, drawing me in and reminding me of my promise to be a good girl from now on.

'Drink!' Frenchy roared. 'You may take the word of Claude Delamere that, however high he rises in the ranks of society, he will never forget his friends.

I gazed around me, through the fug of tobacco smoke, at the glazed eyes, hearing the slurred voices.

And I looked back over my recent history and saw

that this was all the company I deserved, for I had lived a low life – except for one feeble attempt to become honest, which had turned out wrongly through the master and mistress I had come under, and I had not been brave – and so I had sunk as low as possible and had come to this.

'Friends!' the drinkers chorused in answer to Frenchy's last rousing speech.

Then someone sang a ballad from the time of the great Civil War, and soon the room was swaying in time to the tune, and this was how we spent our first night of success, staggering home to our lodgings just before sunrise.

After that, in spite of what he had promised, Frenchy turned his face to the west and never saw his old friends more. He quickly found a house on the Strand; a broad street of fine mansions, one of the best in London, where our neighbours were amongst the most fashionable in town.

'I am lost!' Mary exclaimed, coming and going along corridors, up and down staircases, in and out of the grand drawing-rooms decorated with fine plasterwork, hung with large portraits of men and women in ancient dress.

Frenchy sent her out to dressmakers and jewellers and told her to buy the most expensive items, for he did not want to be put to shame. He talked cruelly to her and said she must not open her mouth in company, for she could not speak like a lady and was to be looked at but not heard.

As for me, he kept Ambrose to guard me still, though he let me go about pretty freely, so long as the African accompanied me. He dressed me finely, but not extravagantly, and said he would call me cousin Charlotte, and that was how I was to be recognised in future.

'Never talk of the past,' he warned. 'Wipe all record of the highway from you memory. Do not speak of robbery and hanging, but only of the latest fashions and visits to the theatre.'

So Mary got her skirt of apricot silk and necklace of pearls, and I will say she outshone many of the high-born women we mixed with, who were pale and insipid beside her and would not say boo to a goose.

Frenchy got his coach and four, his cook and housekeeper, his fine wines from the vineyards of France.

And August rolled into September and the past seemed like a dream.

'Which coat do you like best, Charley?' Frenchy asked me in the room that was his library.

We were there late one afternoon, the sun slanting through the long windows and falling in bright stripes across the rich red Persian rug. I was teaching Frenchy his first letters, as he had grown suddenly determined to rescue himself from his state of parlous ignorance.

However, Frenchy's mind would not settle to the task, and within five minutes he had Ambrose run to fetch him two new coats from his dressing-room – one of dark gold velvet, the other of russet red.

'The red,' I replied.

'Hah, brief and sullen as ever!' he cried. '"The red", she says, through gritted teeth!'

'I answered the question honestly.'

'Do you not prefer the gold?' he went on, trying it again, parading up and down the room. 'I say, Shar-lee, what about this gold?'

Shar-lee. Suddenly, I was back in the haylofts, up in the saddle, riding through the night. I had to blink and look around the room at the books, through the window into the broad street, to remind myself of present reality.

'The red is best,' I said determinedly.

Frenchy stopped and looked me in the eye. 'We have come very far, you and I,' he muttered, as if reading my thoughts. 'You have seen a good deal in your young life, Charley.'

I could think of no answer, so merely lowered my eyes to the book before me.

'Your silence condemns me,' he complained. 'I hear

unspoken barbs and insults. You do not approve. Come, Charley, confess it – you find me cruel.'

'You have what you wanted,' I muttered. 'And Mary is happy.'

'Aye, happy playing with her sparkling jewels. But we must send her out to the country, I think, for she will never be fit to make conversation with the daughters of dukes and ambassadors.'

'And *you* will?' I demanded with a catch in my voice.

'Aye, and you, Charley. You play a part as well as I.' As always, Frenchy drew me into the centre of his schemes. 'I fancy you can play the lady and find yourself a rich husband when the time comes.'

'You have no feelings! You are guided by greed and nothing else!' Unable to stop myself, I jumped up and accused him.

'Wrong!' he replied. 'Power is as strong a spur to me as love of money. I have the Duke of Newcastle under my thumb, the Secretary of State and right-hand man to Sir Robert Walpole. That is my greatest achievement, and my greatest security for the future.'

'You are cold!' I rushed on. 'Cold and heartless. I care not for the Duke of Newcastle and Sir Robert Walpole. But, how many have you killed to arrive where you are?'

'Ah, the lad!' he said, all at once perceiving the cause of my distress. 'The young highwayman – Robert was his name, too, I think.'

I fell silent and sat down with a heavy thud.

'Ah, Shar-lee!' Frenchy breathed. 'I have broken your heart.' He considered me with a wry look before he told me a truth I had known all along. 'But no, you have broken it yourself by running away from me, just as surely as if you had put the gun to Robert Major's chest and fired.'

Sixteen

In which I sample further delights and suffer an unlooked-for surprise. The reader will see me weep after I undergo the greatest shock that flesh is heir to, as the mighty Shakespeare says.

Mary soon tired of her visits to the seamstress, milliner, wig-maker and jeweller. She looked around for another diversion and told Frenchy that she wished to have her likeness made by a portraitist in Mayfair – a Dutchman who had painted the highest in the land.

'It is what ladies do!' she cajoled. 'They dress in their finest clothes and visit the painter's studio, where they sit still for many hours while the man captures their face and figure on canvas.'

'Do as you please,' Frenchy replied. 'But be sure to take Charley and her sour face with you. See if you can raise a smile from the ungrateful wretch!'

So Mary ordered the coach and we travelled forth along the broadways, looking out at a new city I scarcely recognised, of wide green spaces and elegant squares, of horse-drawn carriages bearing coats of arms, of fine gentlemen on horseback and ladies in feathered hats riding gracefully beside.

'Oh!' Mary would exclaim at each fresh sight around every corner. She loved the statues of great kings and the churches of white stone with their pointed spires, the courtyards, the smell of coffee from the salons, the sound of church bells pealing.

When we reached the painter's studio we were greeted with a deep bow from a foreign-speaking man in dark clothes with a plain white collar. In broken English, he bid us be seated in the tall room redolent with the strange, oily smell of what I later found to be the pigment used by the artist.

Mary let herself be arranged in a seat near a window, one hand holding her fan in her lap, the other resting idly on a small table. Our Dutchman directed her to look sideways towards him, so that he caught her in half profile. 'Good,' he said in his short, stuttering voice, taking up his brush. 'A little more this way – good. And so we begin.'

It was our third visit to Van Bulow's studio. Mary sat still as a statue while the painter silently worked at his canvas, and I found that the afternoon heat made me drowsy. A fly trapped inside the window pane distracted the Dutchman, who told me to open the casement and let the insect fly free, which I did.

The breath of air revived me and I longed for a little more relief from the smell of the oil in which the pigment was mixed, so I slipped out of the room on tiptoe and found myself outside on the street, alone for the first time in many weeks.

Gradually, it came to me that this was a rare chance for me to leave Frenchy and to lose myself in the maze of city streets. I might melt away, out of this life of luxury – but to what?

I had laid no plans, possessed nothing other than the clothes I stood in, had not a single friend to aid me. And so I glanced up and down the street in a spin of indecision.

Two ladies walked by, their satin shoes tip-tapping along the stone pavement. A boy in a brown waistcoat and breeches hurried past with a sealed letter in his hand. A carriage stopped and a gentleman alighted.

And then, with my head already spinning from the lure of freedom, I experienced the greatest shock that could be imagined.

'If it isn't Charley Feather!' A figure stepped out from the alley beside the artist's studio. He shook his head, as if in surprised admiration. 'You're quite the lady, ain't you?'

I gasped in wonderment, felt my heart stop with a

thud and had to hold on to the railing for support, for it was as if I was seeing a ghost.

'You never expected to behold me again, did you, Charley?'

My voice had deserted me, so I shook my head and closed my eyes. When I opened them again, Robert Major was still there.

'You left me for dead on the wharf side,' he said with a grin. 'But here I am, a miracle!'

It was the old smile, the old light-heartedness, but I could not respond. My heart fluttered now, as if it was a bird beating its wings against the cage of my ribs.

'Frenchy merely winged me,' Robert explained, bending over me as I struggled to catch my breath. 'I took a bullet in the shoulder, which was not much.'

'Oh!' I cried. 'I cannot say how glad this makes me! I thank God for it, Robert, truly, with all my heart!'

And I embraced him warmly until he eased himself out of my arms and gently made me stand to hear more of what he had to say.

'It was a bleak night when you and the child made your escape from Frenchy,' he murmured.

I nodded. 'Hannah was drowned,' I told him. 'Frenchy rescued me and has held me prisoner since.'

'A strange prison, Charley.' Looking me up and down in my silk gown and my little necklace of pearls, it seemed that Robert did not believe me. 'I have followed and watched. I have seen the house on the Strand.'

'You have followed me?' I echoed, looking at him anew. He was the same as before – tall and lean, only with a severity about him now that was not how I remembered him.

'Every day. I have crept in your shadow when you went with Frenchy to Westminster. I have been there when you walked with the African and rode in the carriage with Mary.'

'And you have blamed me?' I guessed.

'I had expected more of you,' he confessed slowly. 'I believed you had more spirit.'

I frowned then. 'I am biding my time,' I argued.

'Aye, for how long? Until you have found a suitor to woo you and wed you and take you off to his country estate?'

'Never!' I retorted. 'You think too little of me, Robert.'

'On the contrary, I think too much!' Annoyed by this slip which had allowed me a glimpse of his true feelings, he turned away.

'I thought you were dead!' I cried, grasping his hand. 'My heart was broken. And tell me, Robert, do you know how much courage it takes to cast yourself away into a friendless world?'

He was silent then, and more thoughtful, putting his other hand over mine and studying my face in silence.

'Aye, Charley. For I have done it myself!' He sighed at last, then spoke very tenderly. 'And will you leave Frenchy now and come with us?'

'Us?' I repeated, glancing round and seeing for the first time that someone else stood quietly in the alleyway – a small, pale figure waiting obediently until Robert called her forward and I saw that it was Hannah.

'Another miracle!' he teased, drawing the child between us. 'The truth is, Charley, I slid into the water when Frenchy's back was turned and easily fished her out, little sprat that she is.'

Hannah stared at me in my lady's gown, with my hair pinned up and a fan in my hand.

'She thinks you are too grand to be addressed,' Robert smiled.

I wept now for the first time, hiding my face behind my hand and letting the sobs come.

'Charley is glad to see you,' Robert told the child. 'That is why she cries.'

And I felt as though a great burden had been lifted from my shoulders and a tight band released from around my chest.

Then I sniffed back the tears and said, yes, let us go. Then the door of the studio flew open and Mary rushed out to discover me, saying that Frenchy would be angry if I strayed out of her sight, then seeing Robert with Hannah she fell down in the street in a half faint.

We restored her to her senses as best we could, but now the situation was confused, for Mary threw herself on Hannah and hugged her and said she could scarce believe her eyes, and that the girl looked thin and must come home with us and be taken care of.

'Mary,' I said, 'she has lived with Robert these past weeks. He is the one who saved her from drowning.'

Mary drew breath at last. 'It is not right for Hannah to stay with you, Robert,' she argued. 'She needs a woman to guide her. And you know that we live grandly now, and Hannah will want for nothing.'

Robert stood, deep in thought. He noted the way the child had crept up and slid her small hand into Mary's, as of old. 'Tell me, Hannah, would you like to live in a great house with servants?'

'And shall you visit me there, Rob?' the child lisped shyly.

'No, I cannot.'

I saw the tears well, as Hannah looked from Robert to Mary.

'I will look after her as my very own daughter,' Mary promised. 'I will be more than a mother to her.'

Then Robert knelt down beside Hannah and told her slowly and simply that it was time to go home with Mary. 'There will be pretty gowns to wear and a great fire to sit beside. You will learn to sew and sleep on a bed made of feathers.'

At which Hannah said yes, she wished to go home, and Mary lifted her and hugged her anew.

Robert turned to me then and spoke in his old, carefree way. 'And you, Charley, will you return to the pretty gowns and feather beds?'

My whole life flew before my eyes, both past and future, as I thought out my reply, but it was only a second that had passed before I spoke out.

'Not I!' I declared. 'For remember, I am Charley Feather, highwayman, and will bow down to no man!'

Seventeen

In which the reader may be further surprised on several accounts. I face the greatest danger of my life and cannot tell how it will end.

I cannot say how good and free it felt to be back in boys' breeches and out of my cumbersome petticoats.

'Here comes Charley Feather!' girls would cry, hanging out of windows to catch a glimpse of me in my waistcoat and hat.

I swaggered down the street with Robert at my side, stopping to speak with an old acquaintance, or passing the time of day with a pedlar or fishmonger.

'Charley Feather, back from the dead!' they said, grinning. 'Where have you been, my lad? This place has been the duller for your absence!'

I would slap them on the back and wink, say nothing of the true circumstances, then move jauntily on.

'Walk less daintily, Charley,' Robert would remind me when he saw me mince my steps. 'If you want to assume your old character, you must tie back your hair, jut out your chin and blacken your face and hands a little. Employ an oath or two when you speak!'

And so, with Robert by my side, I enjoyed my return to my old identity, brazenly defying whatever consequences it might bring on.

It was at night, however, when I lay in the dark in a bare attic room in the riverside house of one of Robert's old acquaintances, that I had time and occasion for regret.

Then I would call to mind the look of dismay on Mary's face when I told her I would not go back with her to the Strand, and I knew how Frenchy would blame her, and how in any case he planned to banish her into the country because she was not good enough for him now that he was a gentleman with ten thousand guineas in his purse.

'He will beat me black and blue!' Mary had pleaded, her face drained of colour. 'Charley, I dare not think of what he will do!'

But, though I pitied Mary, I could not make this a reason for my return to the gilded cage. And in the night-time I hoped that Frenchy did have a heart that would be moved by the plight of poor Hannah, and that he would treat the two of them with a little kindness, knowing their dismal history.

By day, Robert and I sat in the inns and taverns, waiting for a little honest employment to fall into our hands. We did not look too hard, I confess, for I had sold my pearls and we lived well on the proceeds, though the money would not last for ever.

And what of the feeling I had in my heart for Robert, and his feeling for me? Well, we kept that hidden from one another after our reunion in Mayfair, each thinking perhaps that the moment had passed, and finding it easier and more natural to act as brother and sister, especially now that I had donned the breeches and sported a three-cornered hat.

I did ask him once, however, why it was that he had followed me so close all these months since our chance meeting on the highway in Leicestershire.

He frowned and hummed and hawed, and would not tell me, but I knew by his blushes that it was because I was dear to him, and when I teased and pressed him over it, he did not deny it.

Then I smiled and mentioned it no more.

'Charley, I would have a message delivered to a ship's captain waiting at the Custom House.' So a merchant would employ me thus, while a silversmith entrusted Robert to carry a newly-engraved plate to a grand house. Or else, a doctor would require medicines and I would write down the names of the drugs and run to the dock to buy them from an East Indies man just disembarked after his long voyage halfway around the globe.

And always I would gaze at the tall ships with their furled sails and rigging rattling against the mast, and imagine the roll and heave of the vessels as the mighty ocean waves crashed against their stout sides.

It was after one of these errands to the docks that I brought back startling news to Robert where he supped at an inn called the Fleece on Lamb Street in Shoreditch.

'O'Neill is on the prowl!' I told him without preliminaries, which made Robert choke on his meat and cough and gasp for breath. 'Plommer's men have glimpsed him stumping along on crutches, swearing his revenge against all who have crossed him!'

'You need not fear a crippled man,' Robert assured me after he had recovered from his surprise. 'Especially now that the streets are ruled by Plommer. O'Neill is yesterday's man. Let him skulk and limp along – we will not care.'

But I shook my head. 'It's Mary's blood that he's after. He calls her hussy and says he will reclaim her from the Frenchman, only to kill her for her treachery and throw her body into the Thames!'

'You think we must warn her?' Robert muttered.

'Yes. There is a way of doing it without crossing Frenchy's path.' My mind was working speedily, and I had already partly thought this through. 'You recall the African?'

Robert nodded.

'He is honest. I will seek him out and tell him that Frenchy must hide Mary in the country, and give him the reason. I know that this is to be Mary's fate in any case, but now Frenchy must do it promptly, and not delay.'

The very next day I went out early in the morning to fulfil this mission, taking up a station in the Strand, waiting until Ambrose, looking splendid in a new uniform of dark-red velvet and gold braid, came down the broad steps at the front of Frenchy's house and set off across York Place towards the river.

As soon as he was out of sight of the mansion, I approached him and waited for him to recognise me in my male attire.

'Aye, 'tis Charley!' I assured him, seeing him a good deal startled. 'How is Mary's portrait coming along?'

'My master says she is to go there no more,' Ambrose muttered. 'She stays at home.'

'And the girl, Hannah – is she well?'

'My master takes care of her,' he said guardedly. 'He hopes she proves more faithful than you did.'

I bridled but held my tongue. 'Now, Ambrose,' I said, 'you must warn Frenchy to take Mary and the child out of the city and hide her in the country, for O'Neill threatens to murder her and he must not lay hands on her, else she is dead.'

Ambrose's frown deepened. 'There is evil in this city.' he murmured in his rich, sonorous voice. 'Not far below the surface, forever rising.'

'True, Ambrose. It is like an undercurrent, or rather a tide that cannot be stopped. O'Neill means to harm Mary, but Frenchy can prevent it, if he has the heart.'

'He is angry. He leaves her and goes to dine alone. He is losing his fortune in cards and drinking.'

So I saw that we could not rely on Frenchy to save Mary's neck, and I implored Ambrose to provide the means for her escape. 'She will need a coach to take her away from here, and there must be a house in the country where she may live quietly with Hannah. Bid her take as much money as she can, and whatever jewellery he has given her. Do this, Ambrose, as a blow against the evil that engulfs us!'

'It is to disobey my master,' he protested.

'Aye, but you are no longer a slave, so think like a free man!' I spoke bluntly for time was short, but I felt what I said with all my heart. 'You see that it is right to save Mary, who has done you no wrong. Besides, you may do this quietly and secretly, so that Frenchy never guesses your part.'

He shook his head. 'My heart would carry this secret as a burden for as long as I live.'

And I saw there was such a thing as being too honest, and I went on imploring him, only departing when he promised at least to warn my old friend, Mary, and hoping that Ambrose's conscience would prick him to acting his part in her escape.

We came then to the ninth day of September, four days before the date set for Wild's trial, and the whole city was buzzing with talk.

'They will hang him as a common horse thief, and good riddance!' Men who had lived under Wild's thumb for years gloated in the taverns.

'The presiding judge is Sir Laurence Stead,' said the women. 'There is not a drop of mercy in the man. He would as soon hang a thief as look at him!'

Then a rumour spread that Wild was claiming the support of a man high up in His Majesty's government, and the name of Thomas Pelham-Holles, Duke of Newcastle crept out in whispers.

'Wild boasts that he is in the Duke's service and will be spared the noose,' many men said.

An angry reply filtered down from Westminster that the said Thomas Wild was a blackguard, and the great Duke would not sully his name by associating with the lowest form of life, as the notorious gang leader was known to be.

'Wild will hang,' the Duke's messengers promised. 'He is as good as dead already.'

'Aye, Wild was always a liar,' people concluded. 'He

hopes to save his skin by naming a great man, but where is the evidence?'

Locked in a safe place by Frenchy! think I to myself when I pick up the whisper. I laugh to think that Wild has told the truth for once in his nasty life yet has no hope of being believed.

But the laughter turned sour on my tongue when news broke – not an hour later – that the said villain, Wild, was sprung from Newgate within days of his date with the hangman. Two gaolers were killed, a third dying from a wound in his stomach, delivered by the bloodthirsty monster, Patrick O'Neill, for it was he who had masterminded the escape.

O'Neill, my fearsome friend, had wrenched Thomas Wild from the hangman's grasp.

If you have ever seen a drop of mercury divide and scatter in a glass dish, then that was how men reacted when they heard that Wild was free.

They ran from the taverns back to their lodgings, or under the dark arches of bridges, down alleyways and into cellars, so that by dusk there was no soul left on the streets.

'What shall we do?' I whispered to Robert from the refuge of our attic room overlooking the river.

'Bolt the door until the trouble is past,' he answered grimly. 'They will send out soldiers to recapture the prisoner. Not a man in London will stand by him now.'

'Except O'Neill,' I breathed.

'Aye but, if the soldiers don't take him, then Plommer will,' Robert promised, for he could see how I shook and trembled. 'Come, Charley. Take heart. The gangs have turned against Wild. By morning it will be over.'

Yet I did not know how we would pass the night. The silent, shadowy crossing of every cat on the street made me shiver, the scuttling of rats under the floorboards stopped my heart and made me gasp. Each second seemed a minute, each minute an hour.

'What is that?' I cried out when the stair creaked.

It was past nine o'clock and already pitch dark.

Robert unbolted the door and took a lighted candle to search the house from top to bottom. I could not stay in the attic alone, and so followed him down into the damp cellar, whence you could hear the wash of the Thames against the wharf, and from there into a room at the back of the house, overlooking a small yard leading down to the river.

'There is no one here, Charley,' he soothed, accidentally blowing out the flame as he leaned in to reassure me. 'Wait, I will fetch another.'

I felt the dark prick my skin, the silence swathe me like a thick blanket.

Was that Robert's step climbing the stair? If so, who

made the rattling noise in the street outside? I turned in fear, but could see no more than a blind man.

'Robert!' I called out from the bottom of the stair, where I had groped and felt my way.

I should have stayed silent, for the cry told my enemy where to find me.

There was a crash as a heavy body broke through the door from the street. A snarl as the man pounced, and then a hand came across my mouth and an arm lifted me off my feet.

I fought with all my might, half struggling free and turning to see a face caught in a lamp carried by a second man. And that face was the one I most dreaded – the scarred, staring, half-strangled face of Patrick O'Neill.

Eighteen

Life narrows to a dark point and several souls depart
from their bodies to embark on their longest journey.
The great River Thames plays her part.

Dark death held me in his grasp. I stared at him and it was the shadowy, swollen face of a half-hanged man.

'Release her,' O'Neill ordered his henchman in a hoarse whisper. They let me go while O'Neill put a pistol to my temple. 'Charley Feather, we meet in poor circumstances!'

I felt my heart flutter, then beat again. 'Shoot me if you will!' I declared.

'That is the very reason I hold this gun to your head,' he sneered. 'But first you will tell me where Mary Brazier is holed up.'

I was to die anyway, so why should I aid the brute? I set my jaw firmly shut and waited for the end.

'She is fled from the Strand,' O'Neill continued, holding the lantern close and pressing the gun harder against my head. 'The house is empty, the cowardly Frenchman has taken cover.'

The villain smelled of ale houses, closed, musty rooms and sickness. His ugly face was grimed and swollen.

'I do not know where Mary is,' I declared truthfully, thankful that Ambrose had acted quickly. O'Neill had me against the wall, pushing my head back as far as it would go. My throat was dry, my heart pounding, and I thought each breath would be my last.

'Charley Feather, I have never held any liking for you,' O'Neill wheezed. 'Always too bold and brazen, forever slithering and sliding through life. This time, however, you may be sure that there is no escape.'

'Pull the trigger and be done with it!' his companion urged, backing on to the street through the broken door. I sensed O'Neill's finger tighten around the trigger.

Then, from the darkness outside the ring of yellow light cast by the lantern, Robert threw himself at the murderous villain.

He had crept down the stairs, stealthy as a cat and more silent. But then the house exploded with a great noise as Robert thrust O'Neill off balance and the lame man swore wildly as both gun and lantern fell from his hands.

The light was extinguished. I let out a scream, then threw myself on the weapon so that O'Neill could not grasp it back. Meanwhile, the accomplice rushed in and set upon Robert with a cudgel, so it was two men against one.

Robert's life was now in my hands. I rose from the floor, my hands shaking hard, my fingers fumbling to find the trigger, but in the thick blackness I could scarcely tell friend from foe.

'Run, Charley!' Robert cried as he lay curled on the floor and the blows rained down on him.

I took aim at one of the hulking shapes intent on beating my friend to death. A shot rang out, and yet I had not squeezed the trigger. A man fell backwards and lay still. A second shot was fired, and O'Neill staggered then fell with a heavy thud.

Then all was quiet. A silence so profound that I thought my ears had burst and I was stone deaf, until I heard Robert groan and raise himself and I ran to his aid, stumbling over the dead men to reach him.

Robert groaned again; he was a heavy weight against me as I pulled his arm around my shoulder and raised him to his feet. We looked to the doorway, whence the shots had come.

'Take care with that pistol, Shar-lee, for it is loaded,' Frenchy instructed, for all the world as if we were two gentlemen out on a moor, shooting pheasants. 'You had best give it to me, lad.'

* * *

Robert's face was cut and bruised, his arm wrenched almost out of its socket, and he had a pain in his ribs that would scarce let him breathe.

'Can you walk until we find a physician?' Frenchy asked, brushing aside my exclamations, and taking Robert's other arm. Thus we half carried him out of that house into the street, which should have been crowded with onlookers drawn by the gunshots, but was in fact eerily empty.

'Fortune smiles on you, Charley,' Frenchy said. 'I swear you were on your way to meet your Maker when I came upon the scene!'

'Aye, and you know Fortune has nothing to do with it!' I retorted. 'My guess is that you were watching O'Neill when he came to your house, and so secretly followed him here to discover his business.'

'There's the thanks I get!' Frenchy laughed. 'Take heed of the wench, Robert, and expect no gratitude from her!'

'I dress as a man, and so act like one!' was my quick reply, intended to cheer Robert, who was suffering much from the blows he had received.

'We will take him to the wharf and find a ship's doctor,' Frenchy decided. 'If his ribs are broken, we should not move him far.'

And so we turned down a dark passage and came out upon the riverside, glad to see the flame of torches set in sconces high on the walls, and the twinkle of candles from within the great sailing ships moored there.

By this light I could see that poor Robert's face was much bloodied. 'I fear they have spoiled your handsome looks.' I murmured, offering him a handkerchief from my pocket,

'They would have spoiled more than that if Frenchy had not stepped in,' he reminded me, then said Frenchy and I should set him down beside a coiled anchor chain and seek help without him.

So we left Robert as comfortable as may be and strode along the narrow wharf, calling up to the ships' decks, asking if there was a doctor aboard.

No one was ready to come to our aid, however, and after we had walked some quarter of a mile, Frenchy stopped and said. 'Something is wrong, Charley. It is as if these were ghost ships, without a crew.'

'They have gone to the taverns,' I suggested, but I began to be nervous again.

The creak of the ships' timbers and the slap of the water against the jetties seemed loud. I looked up at a moon half hidden by fast-moving clouds, and then down and along the wharf at the coils of rope and chain, the piles of fishermen's nets and baskets.

'No, they stay quiet aboard ship,' Frenchy surmised. 'Men hide when there is trouble brewing.'

We stood and watched and waited, but the nature of the unrest still eluded us.

'We should go back to Robert!' I decided, uneasy that we had left him alone.

But before we could retrace our steps, a gang of men who had been concealed down the steep steps of the stone wharf burst upon us, appearing one at a time as if from the depths of the black river, or from hell itself, brandishing swords and knives, following their leader, Thomas Wild.

'Hah!' Frenchy's cry mingled surprise with anger. He stood face to face with Wild, who was surrounded by his band of villains. 'I have seen a finer crew in my time!' he mocked. 'Where did you find these men, Master Wild? Did you scrape them from the gutter?'

I will never forget the look in Wild's eyes as he confronted Delamere.

Here was the traitor who had cheated him out of a fortune and robbed him of his great power among the gangs of the city, for indeed these beggars standing before us were ragged and starving, made savage by a life of poverty. And so Wild's gaze would have struck terror in any man but Frenchy, and his teeth were bared, as if in a snarl.

'You will die for this, Delamere!' Wild threatened. 'Slowly, inch by inch, I will draw the breath from your body!'

With a gesture, he ordered his men on, watching as they scuttled to surround us, and Frenchy drew O'Neill's pistol from his belt. Then Wild himself pulled out a gun and the two enemies levelled their aim, ten strides apart, ready to fire.

Then a dozen soldiers dressed in red jackets, shouldering rifles, came running down the alleys, and Wild, seeing the danger, turned away from Frenchy and fired at the first of them, who however escaped the bullet and charged on towards him.

Enraged, Wild flung himself towards Frenchy, who could have shot him dead on the spot, but who instead turned his gun around and struck Wild with the heavy silver butt, so that the one-time scourge and terror of the city streets staggered sideways, lost his footing on the wet stones and plunged into the river.

I run to the edge of the wharf, staring down, waiting for Wild to resurface. And now there is life on the ships and men come running with lanterns, shouting to each other and crying that Wild is in the water and soldiers looking on. A dark head appeared at last, scarce able to stay above water, dashed by waves, choking and crying out. 'I cannot swim, damn you!' Wild yelled, thrashing with his arms.

Beside me, Frenchy let out another exclamation – 'Hah!' – but this time soft and satisfied.

'Who will save him?' I cried, as the head of the man below vanished a second time.

'No one.' Frenchy foresaw the end.

'Our order is not to bring him back alive,' a corporal confirmed.

And so we stood and watched the man drown.

A second time his head comes up, his voice cursing us, his arms splashing helplessly as the waves take him up against the hull of a ship and the blow sends him down into the depths. He comes up once more, further out into the river, looking small, like a piece of dark flotsam carried on the current. He does not cry out, and no man moves to save him as for the third and final time Thomas Wild disappears from sight.

Monday 30 September, 1739

I have seen Dick Turpin hang on the Knavesmire and the notorious Thomas Wild drown in the great River Thames, and that is enough for any man or woman in this year of Our Lord, 1739.

'So, Charley,' Mary begins, as Hannah plays contentedly among some chicks scratching the earth by the cottage door. 'You have put by your fine feathered hat for good?'

I rustle my skirt and dip her a curtsey. 'Aye, for good or ill,' I reply, for I am not certain of the future, and who can be in these turbulent times?

I only know that I have abandoned my hat and breeches for Robert's sake, and that Mary is safe with the child, and happy with her lot. She lives quietly, out of society, in a house where the stone floors are scrubbed daily and the limed walls are white as freshly-laundered linen.

'And you do not pine after Frenchy?' I ask her in turn.

We watch Robert invite Hannah to sit by his side in the shade of a great chestnut tree.

'Sometimes,' Mary confesses with a sigh. 'But I hear he lives a loose life, and will come to no good.'

'He has fallen into gambling, his creditors already hammer at his door,' I tell her. 'He has led us a dance, Mary, but he has saved us too, so I am sorry he does not make the best of his lot.'

'And Ambrose stays at his side?'

'Aye. The African will not forsake him.'

I tell her that the last time I saw Frenchy was in the light of flaming ships' torches, when Wild drowned and Frenchy saluted me and departed with a flourish, as of old. 'So, Shar-lee, it is over and I wish you *bon voyage*!'

The tide dragged Wild's body out to sea, and Frenchy, my scourge and saviour, vanished from my life.

'Charley, Mary, come and tell us what Hannah has found!' Robert calls us. We see through the chinks of her fingers a tiny creature with a sharp nose and twinkling black eyes. It is brown and furry, smaller than a mouse.

' 'Tis a vole,' Mary says.

'A shrew!' I counter.

The creature nips Hannah's finger with her sharp teeth. She shrieks and lets her go. I sit under the tree beside Robert, while Mary takes Hannah indoors to dress the small wound.

'You are wistful?' he asks.

I shake my head. 'No, I am glad to go, only sorry to leave Mary and Hannah.'

'It will be a new life,' Robert promises, taking my hand and together we gaze out across the green English countryside, at the rolling hills and the trees turning golden under the blue autumn sky.

There is an ocean to cross and a continent to explore. We will work our passage, Robert and I.

I picture him climbing the rigging, peering out from the crow's nest of the *Eleanor May*. I am to help the ship's doctor by writing down the names of medicines and by nursing those who fall sick on the voyage.

We are to sail to America, which is to say, into the vast unknown.

'Tomorrow, Charley,' Robert murmurs, holding me fast.

'Aye, tomorrow,' I say with a sigh.